# The **Misadventures** of
## Wunderwear Woman

## **Denis Hayes**

PARTRIDGE
A Penguin Random House Company

ISBN:       Hardcover            978-1-4828-9647-3
            Softcover            978-1-4828-9646-6
            Ebook                978-1-4828-9648-0

**To order additional copies of this book, contact**
Toll Free 800 101 2657 (Singapore)
Toll Free 1 800 81 7340 (Malaysia)
orders.singapore@partridgepublishing.com

www.partridgepublishing.com/singapore

# The Adventures of Wunderwear Woman

Wunderwear Woman knew without looking in a mirror that she was a big girl. She felt that she was really a slim girl trying to burst out. At times she did nearly burst out but she wasn't slim. She sensibly realised that she was the equivalent of two slim girls trying to get out but felt that this should be suppressed. It could make her seem schizophrenic. Which one would really be her and which one should her friends talk to?

She consoled herself by going to shops that called her large, outsize, mature or just "Big Girl".

She earned her nickname from the fact that she was always wondering what to wear and championed vpl, vbs, and camel toe. That is she showed a visible panty line, visible bra straps and as for camel toe, well her clothes fitted her so tightly that she had no choice but to show in outline what should in all modesty have best been concealed.

But whatever, she felt magnificent.

"She felt magnificent"

She refused to be tattooed even though tattoo artists told her she had great acreage that just begged for it. She thought it was common and a bit dirty.

Only celebs and wannabees had tattoos.

How could such a well endowed but unlikely lady become a hero?

All the female heroines were slim, ultra hard bodied and very, very intense and screwed up. They also wore funny clothes the wrong way round.

She thought long and hard and decided to look about to see what wrongs she could right. It would be her mission to seek out unfairness and try to straighten it out.

"Yeah, go girl, go put the world right!"

She told her friends and they all shouted, "yeah, go girl go, put the world right."

She listened. That's what she would do, she would put the world right. She looked earnestly at her colleagues and sounded off triumphantly, "yeah it's simple enough. The opposite of right is wrong. But wait a minute another opposite is left. Hmm, not so obvious. Never mind, I will fight against both of them."

Then she stopped short and faced a reality check.

She didn't have any amazing powers. She was in fact quite ordinary. A bright enough, big enough, nice enough girl, but ordinary.

She hadn't been born on another planet confused by kryptonite. She had been bitten by insects but none of them had managed to help her stick on walls or ceilings. She traced her ancestry but found no demi-gods, only good natured eccentric aunts who had left her a lot of money. She researched Kung Fu gurus but didn't manage to trace any who were living who could run up the side of high rise buildings or catch bullets in their mouths. Those who had tried, died.

So she tried a more modern, technical approach.

She blogged, she twittered and she shoved herself onto Facebook offering her services to anyone who required them.

She asked, "have you been wronged? Then I will right it. Are you right but gone left then I will sort you out. Call me. Ask for my services. I am Wunderwear Woman."

She got no replies except from perverts who demanded more in the way of services than she was prepared to give.

She walked the streets looking for opportunities but only got more offers from perverts.

Where were the righteous downtrodden millions who would jump at her offer of help?

In desperation she decided to accept a few visits from the perverts to see what they wanted and help them by trying to straighten them out. Unfortunately after a few minutes of their company Wunderwear's idea of help was to crunch their balls and beat them up. Regrettably this didn't straighten them out at all but doubled them over. She was shaken when she discovered that most of them loved it and wanted more.

One of the most persistent, Holy Joe as he called himself, told Wunderwear, "I'm only doing this to get nearer to God. God forgives a sinner you see so please strip me naked, tie me up, throw me in a sack and beat me while I masturbate and praise The Lord."

That was not at all inspiring so Wunderwear just beat him up.

She didn't want to be charitable to drunks, addicts and chocoholics. There was help enough for them already. As for necrophiliacs, nymphomaniacs, kleptomaniacs and megalomaniacs, well with names like that they were beyond all hope let alone help. If you couldn't pronounce the name how could you understand the problem? Obviously they were called those impossible names on purpose so that helpers would stumble at the first hurdle and give up. Paedophiles could be simply dealt with. Shoot them.

Where were the normal people with normal problems?

Perhaps the normal people didn't have problems that needed her help.

She thought again. She would go on the campaign trail.

Her first campaigns were not successful. She petitioned airlines to provide wider seats for wider people but couldn't tell them how wide was wider because there always seemed to be someone who was wider still!

She cajoled restaurants, bars and cafes to abandon bucket seats or fixed benches too close to the table but was told to get lost and go and stick her nose into her own business or words to that effect.

While campaigning she noticed that slim people looked down their noses at her size and didn't seem to sympathise at all. So she first tried the silent approach by fixing a stare on them challenging them to eat more and exercise less.

When that didn't get her message across then she tried a more verbal approach accusing them of insipidness, weakness and anorexia. That obviously was not helpful as they got quite insulting and used unflattering words to describe her.

Slowly it sunk in that this was not the way forwards.

Her feelings had been hurt by the remarks directed at her so she decided to fight back. But how?

She could stick up for herself all right but it wasn't her style to go around thumping people because of their size. She could try reasoning but she did notice that people's eyes tended to glaze over whenever she went into her style of long winded explanations.

She despaired a little. How on earth was she going to right wrongs and make the left go right when she couldn't get past first base?

First off she would deal with her own feelings.

# Political Correctness

She asked around and was put in touch with a group of intense people who described what had happened to her as political incorrectness.

Political correctness would cure all the ills in society they told her.

She asked them where their church was and got a funny look.

"So you're not religious then?" she babbled on, "funny that. You're so full of fervour, so sure you're right, and I'm against the left by the way as it's the opposite of right, and you say you're right, so if you're not religious you must be politicians, 'cos they always say they're right even when they're wrong and ---- ." Wunderwear faded out needing to take a breath, looked around to see a number of faces staring blankly at her.

"hmmmpf," she went, "OK, where do I start?"

She found only lukewarm, hesitant support from her friends who felt that Big Brother had gone too far. This did not deter her.

"Look," she said, "you obviously don't understand. Being politically correct means that ordinary people can tell politicians how to behave doesn't it? Come on now, that must be a good thing to support."

To her horror she saw her friends convulsed with laughter.

"You wish," they shouted, "it doesn't mean that at all. It means that the politicians tell YOU how to behave with hundreds more moronic robotic bureaucrats spying on everyone absolutely determined to find insults.

Not only that, interfering nosy busybodies set themselves up to be judge and jury, the ultimate thought police, causing the real police to get even more confused about what they're doing. So everyone becomes a hypocrite because they are too scared to say what they really think and feel. Not good."

"OK," thought Wunderwear, "not good, think again girl. Maybe you've found a great campaign in the making. Undo political correctness and bring back political incorrectness. Oh shit! Wait a minute, isn't that what hurt my feelings in the first place? I'd better think this through."

Wunderwear was a resourceful gal. She told the Intense Earnest People, "Dear IEP's I appreciate what you're saying but I reckon I can sort out the bad from the good without being told, just like most people. Political correctness means to me that everyone is being threatened with punishment for stating a possible contrary opinion. No reasoning, just force.

No partially confused police force just a totally confused one. No guilty criminals anymore only misunderstood victims, who always claim they were abused as children."

"Oh no, that's not what we mean," said Mr. Most Intense, "disagreement yes, but it must be stated in a non offensive way. There's a way of saying things you know."

"Oh yeah and only you know how to say it is that it? If I have been insulted in a most inoffensive way it's still bloody offensive. If I find someone obnoxious then I just love to be offensive. I feel good!" exclaimed Wunderwear.

"Not a very nice attitude," said Earnest, "However you must understand that no one is forced to say things they don't want to."

"What about sending in policemen against screwed up armed murderers and making them yell out 'armed police' and other things before being allowed to do anything?" asked Wunderwear, "it's not a silly schoolgirl game you know?

The police, ambulance and fire brigade are the only one's running towards trouble when everyone else, including you, are running the opposite way to safety.

What about admitted killers getting off because a Judge says a wrong word in summary? What are you doing about that?"

"We are more concerned with inter-relationships and socio-economic causes," came the answer, "That's progress in a civilised society, you know?"

"People aren't politically correct," answered one intense chubby man.

"In the meantime the uncivilised one's are killing more of us than ever before," shrieked Wunderwoman.

"Yes but that's because people aren't politically correct," answered one intense chubby man. That's because they still have to put up with insults and stereotypes."

"No it's not" said Wunderwear, "it's because you tell them their rights all the time and never tell them their wrongs. Particularly immigrants. They no longer want to integrate, they want to take over and have preference because of you. There are no go areas in my country and that's not me being racist, it's a criminal fact. You play right into the hands of the extremists. Anyhow if a thug beats up a seventy year old lady to steal her pension and handphone he is an out and out shitty thief isn't he?"

"Is he?" said Chubby smarmily, "who is the real victim I wonder?"

"The old lady, of course, you bloody moron," she exclaimed, completely exasperated.

"If a supermarket puts stuff out on their shelves a normal person thinks it says buy me. Only a criminal thinks it says steal me. If you ask me, I think you lot aren't wired up right."

"My goodness," exclaimed Wunderwear, "if someone calls me a fat slob and I retaliate with skinny git we're both guilty. If a guy flirts with me a few times then I can claim harassment and no one will flirt with me. What a stupid world.

No fun and less banter. We have dumb women who take twenty years to make up their minds to decide if they've been raped or not. Not as dumb as you think because they only seem to make up their minds when the guy has become rich and famous. They always claim they do it for women everywhere. Ha bloody ha! Only Oprah would fall for that. Yuk!"

Wunderwear was really getting wound up. She was partly aware that she was sounding priggish and self righteous at the same time but was past caring.

"Anyway how would you stereotype me? Don't answer that!!"

"You don't understand," chubby said pompously. "Look you're a woman. Half the people in the world are women but how many are there in positions of power. The same with race and colour. We need proportionate quotas, and we will get them if we have to prosecute everyone to do it."

"Yes I'm a woman but I'm not a bloody quota," she screamed, "I want equality based on ability not privilege. If you want more women in parliament or the cabinet then tell them to get elected and earn it. That would really piss off the men."

"What are you going to do in North, South and East Africa. Going to have a bleedin' hard job finding a quota of white men based on world proportions there aren't you?" she demanded, "and as for India and China—well!!"

"You've got the whole world queueing up to be offended. Lawyers even invent new ways and reasons to be offended so that they can earn fees from ridiculous cases that could have been solved by a smile, commonsense or a witty put down in the first place."

"Good result!? Nah, not the way to go, things need doing but not in that blind, blundering way. Convince me don't criminalise me. See yah guys."

# The Chef's Choice

As Wunderwear seemed really wound up her friends decided they should meet at a really posh restaurant in West London, north of the river of course. People like Wunderwear and crowd only rarely ventured south of the Thames. They did so just for the sole purpose of living dangerously. Going anywhere near Tottenham or West Ham was bad enough but going South was beyond the pale. They could believe that the people there were the salt of the earth but why did they have to be so common.

They only came in touch with them when they hurried their way through the southern suburbs on their way to visit their refined friends and relatives in Surrey arriving with a great sense of relief.

"Do you know that some of the waitresses here are the daughters of the aristocracy?" asked one of her friends, "they do it as a sort of gap year."

"A gap between what?" asked Wunderwear, "between bed and brain?

Come on they're all just Sloanies aren't they?"

"What's a Sloany?" asked one of the girls.

"Oh god help me," exclaimed Wunderwear, "a Sloany is a Sloane Ranger, one of those unemployable rich girls too posh to do hard work and too dumb to do technical stuff. They usually end up marrying useless Hooray Henrys. Well suited. They spend all their lives together thinking they are superior, riding horses and looking down their noses at others."

"Like what we do?" laughed a friend.

"Exactly," smiled Wunderwear, "but without the horses. Can't keep them in the kitchen. They always shit and pee in the wrong places. Do it on purpose if you ask me."

"Let's go in."

Conversations were subdued to match the minimalist decor and subdued lighting.

They were directed to their table by a rosy cheeked young lady using hand signals and affirmative smiles.

"Is she deaf and dumb or something?" asked Wunderwear wonderingly.

"SSSHH," hissed one of the girls, "they don't say very much so as not to spoil the ambiance for the diners."

"I can see this is going to be a real rave this is," moaned Wunderwear, "haven't they got any music."

"They're playing some, can't you hear? It's background music."

"God, I'm either going deaf or the background is so far away it's over the bloody horizon," she said.

"Are you going to be like this all night or are you going to try and be positive for goodness sake?" asked a friend in exasperation.

"Positive!"

"Right then, please sit down and be quiet."

"Okay."

They managed to order from a haughty, well preserved, middle aged lady without too much fuss by looking daggers at Wunderwear every time she looked as though she was about to explode.

The menu was as minimalist as the decor and so were the helpings of food. More style than substance.

Starters were successful, cleared away and the main course arrived.

The sauce, or gravy, was served separately to the food. Wunderwear looked at it and called over one of the waitresses. They all had that magic manner of being pleasant at the same time as looking as though they had a bad smell under their noses.

"I'm a bit shakey," explained Wunderwear, "could you be kind enough to pour that on for me?"

"I beg your pardon," said the woman, seemingly surprised.

"Pardon granted," smiled Wunderwear and then spelled out her words slowly and clearly, "could you pour that gravy in there all over my din dins here. I would be much obliged."

The waitress drew herself up haughtily and said in her most fruity voice, "the last time I was asked and did such a thing was for Lord Snowden and Princess Margaret."

She waited for the re-action calmly while Wunderwear's friends held their breath.

"Are they here tonight?" she asked.

"No, of course not," came the puzzled reply.

"Good, so you won't have any problem doing it for me now then, will you?"

The waitress shrugged her slim shoulders and dutifully poured as requested.

"The upper classes are always slow to catch on. That's why they stick the number one son in the City, the number two in the Church and any women they might have in the Countryside. They used to send their eldest son to the Army but nowadays they don't get killed off quickly enough." Wunderwear explained a little too loudly.

No one gave any evidence of having heard the remark although one or two titters were heard from neighbouring tables. Whether in sympathy or contempt could not be determined.

"You do realise that the people here are quite, quite remarkable, don't you?" said Naomi importantly.

"How?" asked Wunderwear.

"Their ancestors go back for ever, such old families. Incredible isn't it?"

"Oh my god, how awesome," Fiona breathed reverently.

Wunderwear burst out laughing, "you are a right pair of bimbos aren't you? Of course they go back for ever or they wouldn't be here now, would they? We all do. Everyone of us here now goes back for ever because our ancestors did all that begetting bit over and over from the beginning of time. Those who didn't aren't here now, are they? We are all related to each other and that Lucy or whatever who came out of Africa. So tuck in cousins before our next nearest relatives the chimps take over."

They had just started to tuck in when Wunderwear stopped, looked around, and called over their luckless waitress.

"Yes madam, how can I help?" she asked.

"Yes madam, how can I help?"

"Where's the salt and pepper?" Wunderwear asked, "we haven't got any here. Can we have some?"

To Wunderwear's surprise she seemed at a loss over such a simple request and disappeared out the back.

She re-entered with a beautifully coiffeured and stunningly dressed elderly woman. They came up and stood either side of Wunderwear.

"Yes, can I help you?" asked the woman.

"Yes, simple really, obviously a bit too simple. I would just like to have some pepper and salt please. Is that okay with you?" asked Wunderwear a little facetiously.

"Why?" came back the rather surprising answer.

"Why? Why do I want some pepper and salt? Well the salt's not to throw over my shoulder for luck and it's not to make that fish on the plate feel more at home. It's to season the food. You know spice it up a little. Humans have been doing it for donkeys years. In fact even flies love it," said Wunderwear with the sort of smile she saved for when she had to explain things to those retards in the creative section at work.

"We don't have any for the tables. We don't wish our discerning diners to use them," said the woman.

"Why on earth not, what's the matter with pepper and salt? Love it on fish and chips."

"I'm sure you do," said the woman, "but our chef does not work for a Chinese takeaway on the corner of any old high street, he is GERARD."

"Right, I get the bit that he shows off on TV but what's that got to do with pepper and salt?"

"Gerard ensures that he adds just the right amount of seasoning to any dish, any changes he regards as sacrilege. It is all decided for you by the expert that he is. It is what you pay for," she said smugly.

"When he leaves tonight does he dress in nice clothes that suit his taste and is exactly what he paid for?" asked Wunderwear.

"Well yes, but ---."

"Right then, I won't tell him how to dress and what he should like and pay for when going out to play. So you explain to him that he shouldn't tell me what I should like and pay for when I go out to eat, okay?

Now please get me the bloody salt and pepper."

Wunderwear's friends' mouths were all agape.

"Look and learn girls, look and learn," she said.

They were all quiet for a while until Naomi ventured with, "what do you think of that brave women who had both her breasts off?"

"God, I know," said Fiona, with awe, "imagine. A double masectomy."

They looked expectantly at Wunderwear who didn't say a word.

"Her partner supported her, wasn't that lovely," said Naomi.

Wunderwear looked up, "good job it wasn't me then. Lop my boobs off and there wouldn't be much of anything left to support would there?" She went back to her chewing.

Her friends looked at her stomach and backside but decided to keep quiet.

"Why did she do it anyway? Was she dying of cancer?" asked Wunderwear. Terrible disease that, lot's of treatments. Suppose that none worked and she had to have them off, right? My heart really goes out to those women. A horrible decision to have to make."

"Well no actually," said Fiona, "she didn't have anything wrong with her at all. There was a bit of family history so she decided to have them off anyway."

Wunderwear slowly looked up. "Do you mean to say she had her tits off when there was nothing wrong?"

"Do you mean to say she had her tits off when there was nothing wrong?"

"Well yes," said Naomi, "but there was a chance, so she thought."

"Doesn't seem much thought there to me. Maybe nothing wrong with her body but there was something wrong with her brain," exclaimed Wunderwear.

"How can you be so heartless?" cried Fiona, "she might have got it later."

"So what?" said Wunderwear, "then you get treatment don't you. I might get appendicitis 'cos my brother did but I don't go and have my appendix out just in case do I? Overian Cancer can hit any woman, it's like that you know, but I'm not going to have my ovaries out until I have to. A lot of men get prostate cancer but they don't go and get their dicks cut off early just in case do they?

Her friends eyes grew wider so Wunderwear thought she had better make a grand finale.

"Look," she said, "both my parents died when they were sixty years old but I'm not going to commit suicide now because it may happen to me then, am I? Nobody knows the future. Daft way of thinking to my mind."

Wunderwear sniffed, looked to see if there was any further dissent and seeing none she tucked in heartily to what was left of her meal.

Her friends appeared to have lost some of their appetite.

They all used a fair bit of salt though!

# Political Leanings

As she had learned the word political she decided to involve herself in politics. After all she was there to right wrongs.

She found out that the "Right" supported her suggested PC reforms but realised that they wanted to chuck everything out altogether. No rights for others. The rights they wanted were for themselves or no rights for anyone at all.

So she went "Left" and found that too many wanted to go to even more extremes of PC, some so silly that they were contradictory and often self-defeating.

She consulted her friends, "look guys is the Left right or is the Right right? The Right is never left and some would say was seldom right either. However the Left is sometimes right although they're left. See, I'm confused."

Her friends admitted she had confused them as well.

She changed her mind. She would leave that one to others.

What's a gal to do though?

The answer came to her when out with her friends one evening just before they became so drunk that everything and everyone made wonderful sense and seemed so clever.

They were horrified at the amount of random shootings in the "good ole US of A." School, mall, drive by and drug killings were so commonplace.

What was the single unifying factor—a gun.

So that's an easy one thought Wunderwear. Ban guns and more people get to live.

Simple folks—let's do it.

Wunderwear Woman to the rescue. If guns were wrong then they must be part of a Left wing or Socialist plot because the Right always said that anyone who was wrong was left and a Socialist. The Right must be right.

So if banning weapons was right then get the guilty Left to reform the gun laws.

Wunderwear was astounded to find that the Left wanted to do just that.

The Right didn't. So the Right was Wrong. Oh dear.

Those good 'ole boys wanted desperately to hang onto their toys. "Give everyone a gun and we'll all be safe, 'cos those bad guys keep popping up and us good guys should be able to pop 'em off whenever we can. Have one hell of a shoot out at the schools. Good for the kids, in fact give the kids guns, beats watching Rambo on TV."

"Actually," Wunderwear thought, "the Right are downright ignorant when it comes to a discussion. Instead of talking common sense they keep on quoting something about their rights under an amendment to the US Constitution."

Wunderwear investigated.

She found that the amendment was written about 250 years ago by upper class British rebels in the colonies who didn't like their German King.

The British in Britain didn`t like him much either but they didn't tell everyone to go around blasting automatic weapons at little kids hundreds of years later. Compared to today they only had popguns anyway. Deadly but after one shot everybody could get out of range before a reload. Try running away from a submachine gun with a full magazine held by some lunatic exerting his rights to rebellion made in a society that no longer exists.

"An amendment written by upper class British Rebels upset with their German King about 250 years ago."

Are these people screwy or what?

Wunderwear jokingly told them to go and dress up and be daft enough to act it all out again only to find that they did.

Gentle Jesus said, "suffer the little children to come unto me," but I don't think he quite meant that!

Gentle Jesus said, "suffer the little children," but I don't think he meant that!!

Wunderwear came to the conclusion that it had little to do with amendments which could be amended but more to do with selfish macho ignorance.

So Wunderwear tackled the Left again.

Oh dear, they mainly agreed with her.

So was the Left right again.

But some of the Left were wrong because they supported the Right.

She found that there were perfectly decent people on Left and Right and there were also the silly shitheads who seemed to be everywhere.

She was told it was all a question of education. Educated people would do good.

Yeah, well Hitler and his gang were educated weren't they? They were certainly good all right. Good at wiping out whole areas of population that they had decided were dispensable. They eventually succeeded in decimating their own people. So much for their education.

Others advocated religion but one lot had burnt people at the stake for years a long while ago and another lot were blowing up everybody and everything now. So much for goodness, mercy, kindness, tolerance and understanding.

Poor old Wunderwear.

She was finding that once you try to escape from your cocoon then all hell breaks loose.

# A Simple Shoe in

Things were not working out so Wunderwear did the only thing that a sensible girl could do when confused.

A large dose of Shopping Therapy was needed.

And therapy was best shared with friends.

SMS call ups went out and within a short period of time a small group had collected at their local Starbucks ready to up and go after being fortified with a fair dose of caffeine.

Way to go girls!

And away they went.

They were a motley crew of assorted shapes and sizes.

The glamour girls made a beeline for Victoria's Secret.

They all crammed into the shop.

Wunderwear Woman looked for a place to sit down. This was not a place for her and the shop assistants knew it.

She and another couple of large scale friends were ignored.

Most of the panties would not have made a decent wristband on Wunderwear and as for the bras—well—maybe they would have just barely obscured a nipple.

An assistant came up to see if she could be of help, probably out of guilt.

She held up a flimsy g-string and asked what madam thought of it, would it suit her? She emphasised the thong by stretching it and admiring the tiny v shaped frontpiece.

Wunderwear told her that when she was sunbathing and needed something to protect her nose she would call her. The assistant beat a hasty retreat. She returned to the excited group continually picking up, holding up and gushing with admiration at anything they felt to be more sexy than others.

Wunderwear was astounded at what her slim friends were buying. She knew they were slim but the scanty bits of material they were snapping up certainly wouldn't cover what little they did have.

She asked one married friend what her husband thought of such sexy stuff.

The friend looked at Wunderwear as though she was not sure whether she was joking or not.

She said her husband had not noticed what she was wearing for years. He was strictly the usual "let's get 'em off, let's get it in, let's get it done and let's get it over quick," type. She was not buying the sexy underwear for her husband's benefit, it was for her boss at work. She knew how to arouse him and he knew how to make it last and they couldn't wait to do it again.

Wunderwear took a closer look at the panties. They could do all that?

Nah! Too small! Pity??

She was a woman of larger appetites.

Wunderwear took a closer look at the panties, "could they really do all that?"

She and the rest of the bigger ladies were growing impatient. Where were the clothes for them?

Their slim friends joked and said that they would eventually get to the camping shops and not to worry as hot air ballooning was becoming fashionable.

Very funny! Their jokes were as corny as their feet.

Wait a minute—feet? Shoes?

Yeah.

She knew that big muscles and a big head meant a little dick but big bums and huge tits didn't mean big feet.

Wunderwear knew she had good feet as she managed to see them once or twice a year when she cut her toenails. One hell of a struggle!

Let's go!

The shoe shop was more of an even playing field.

There were five or six women reviewing about one hundred pairs of shoes and still couldn't make up their minds.

They turned the shop upside down then they asked the assistant if that was all there was!!?? What else was there? Any new arrivals?

They were told that they had seen the lot so they let their disapproval show by grimacing and other facial contortions. They seemed on the verge of walking out without buying.

Only a lunatic would work in a women's shoe shop.

Wunderwear and friends however were in a buying mood.

Within minutes six inch heels were on half a dozen pairs of feet. Little used calf muscles were bulging to the limit with toes packed into confined spaces and full body weight stacked up behind.

Human heels soon came back down to earth.

Wunderwear concluded that extra high heels were for featherweights not heavy weights.

She favoured her big battered trainers but didn't dare say so. However she got cunning. There was a delightful pair of Zanotti shoes that looked and felt like trainers but they had inbuilt high heels just right.

Paradise.

Expensive but exclusive. She wore them straight away.

She suffered a twinge of conscience. How was this putting wrongs to right?

She consoled herself by thinking that she had kept some poor Third World peasant in food for another day only to find out that they were made in Italy.

Well Italy wasn't doing so well was it? Perhaps they were made in the South of the country under Mafia protection.

Yeah she felt better.

But she also felt she should be into more serious stuff.

She felt she should be into more serious stuff.

# Another World

What about this Third World.

Where was it for a start?

She wasn't too good at geography but knew enough to understand that it wasn't on a different planet even if the poor people felt it was.

She also understood that it wasn't to be found in a fake African setting in a designer brand advert with two celebrities gazing heroically into a future that third world members would never share. Their free perks would be prominently displayed of course with not a starving kid in sight.

So where was it?

She had saved a bit, but was a bit enough to transport her to another world?

She started reading the newspapers, watching CNN and other news channels in the hope of getting clues.

She tried the History Channel but stumbled onto repeat after repeat of fruit and nut cases proving we were really aliens while at the same time being invaded by them and in danger of extermination.

At times she was encouraged by some of the optimism shown in a series only for every episode to end with a but. The but was that disaster was just about to happen.

She tried animal and geographic channels but it appeared that everyone and everything was always on the verge of extinction.

She came to the conclusion we all lived in the Third World.

She was fascinated by CNN. It was obvious that all their reporters, particularly the weather ones, were paid by how many words they could utter loudly in the space of seconds. The words poured out, with complete conviction but utterly without expression, repeated over and over in slightly different ways time after time at more than a hundred breathless miles an hour.

This was probably because the producers realised that no one could pick up on the rapid fire talk first time so it all had to be part of a repetitive cycle. Well how else could you fill up a news channel with news 24 hours a day.

Because they were incapable or afraid of coming to any conclusion they produced all kinds of so called experts to confuse the subject even more and eventually cut off everything before a resolution by running out of time.

She found that breaking news broke faster on BBC than it did on others while Al-Jazeera showed much more rounded view points but biased. Poor old Israel fighting for it's very existence everyday always got a bad break. So much for the so called powerful Jewish Lobby in the USA which was always trotted out by opponents when convenient, totally ignoring hundreds of other Lobbyists campaigning all the time. As they say, never let the truth get in the way of a good story.

Slowly she put all the pieces together.

Most of the Third World was East apparently.

She came to the conclusion that we all lived in the "Third World."

This puzzled Wunderwear because New York was East of Chicago and Chicago was East of San Francisco. London was East of New York and so on until she came back to the start. Even then she was still going East.

The West was even more puzzling because the East objected to being ruled by the West and didn't want to copy them.

However Saudi Arabia was West of Malaysia yet Malaysia seemed determined to copy the Saudis and some wanted to be ruled by Saudi rules.

Yet Pakistan was West of Bangladesh and the Banglas had shown they definitely didn't want to be ruled by Pakistan.

Australia and New Zealand were East of almost everywhere but were called Western.

So really none of this labelling made sense.

Wunderwear came to a decision. She would find out in each country why the poor were poor, and where the money was going and why.

It took no time at all.

Blind faith, unchallenged corruption, cronyism and incompetence was the order of the day nearly everywhere that wasn't West.

However there was one hell of a lot of poor, elderly and underprivileged in the West so what was their excuse?

But she had already found out that the West did not exist.

Wunderwear gave up before she got her oversize knickers in a complete twist.

There just had to be something.

East, West, Left, Right, Up and Down, Round and Round,
so confusing.

# A Model Career

Before she could launch herself in a new direction she was invited to a fashion show by one of her friends who was a model.

Wunderwear was wondering. Could she be a model? She felt she was a magnificent specimen of womanhood and indeed she was. All 250 lbs of her.

She was an hour glass shape, just a big glass that's all, not pear shaped like a lot of them.

But?

Models were all miserable looking stick insects who walked with weird exaggerated steps down the catwalk. They had obviously learned the method from the Monty Python School of Funny Walks. As for the clothes, surely the designers were taking the piss and showing their intense dislike of women. There was never anything on show that a girl like Wunderwear could wear with confidence. In fact she couldn`t even get her fist in one of the trouser legs of skinny jeans. What a name to give them anyway. "Skinny."

Prejudice, that's what it was!

Once upon a time if a girl said she was a model then she was looked at with awe and respect. Now she was looked on with shock and sympathy and surprise if she hadn't shown her bare tits on page three or appeared nude in a magazine at some time or other.

Wunderwear felt good for herself and bad for them.

She didn't feel quite so sure when she arrived at the show.

The first woman she bumped into seemed anorexic.

"Wow, you're so skinny you must be a model, have you been in rehab yet?"

Wunderwear exclaimed, "wow you're so skinny you must be a model, have you been in rehab yet?"

The glassy eyed woman stubbed out the sweet smelling ciggie smouldering in her mouth, stuck it into her Louis Vuitton handbag, and shoved past Wunderwear with surprising strength.

"Well whatever," exclaimed Wunderwear, "some people have no manners."

She went and sat down in her reserved seat and wished that her campaign for seats for bigger butts had been more successful.

She turned to the woman next to her, looked her over, and came to the conclusion that facial surgery alone had kept some practitioner in expensive call girls for years.

She knew that ultra rich people invented names that only they could use. Escorts were not prostitutes, whether male or female, because they said that there was no obligation for sexual activity to take place. After all it could just be a fun night out.

Wunderwear chuckled to herself, "oh yeah, go tell that to the marines."

The woman looked at her questionally.

"Nice surgery," observed Wunderwear obligingly, "how often do you have to have it fixed?"

The woman looked straight through her.

"Miserable old cow," thought Wunderwear, "bet she hasn't had it for years."

That thought stopped her dead in her tracks. When had she last had it?

In fact when had she ever had it without some disaster overtaking her.

She wasn't cold, no way. If anything she was a little too enthusiastic and when she got worked up, which was quick and easy, she was inclined to take over.

If only she could have attracted a body builder or Sumo wrestler she would have been fine but it was usually the wimps who wanted her because they felt the need to dominate a big woman.

The big guys fancied the little women for the opposite reason.

Wunderwear could easily and swiftly warm up, then get impatient as the little fella tried to find his way in especially when he couldn't get it up laying on top. The distance was often just too far.

Wunderwear always got fed up with him puffing and panting in mid air so would decide to roll over and get on top. Invariably she would lose him. She knew he would be in there somewhere but GPS was not yet designed for such situations. She would grope about underneath her until she managed to pull his flattened head out far enough to plonk a big kiss on his gaping mouth. Most times this passionate gesture had to turn into a kiss of life.

Wunderwear found this to be most unsatisfactory but never found out how the little fellas felt because they were usually in a state of shock for weeks and never called her again.

She tried once or twice to make contact after which one had a nervous breakdown and the other voluntarily declared himself insane.

She looked hopefully around the packed audience but from the body language and fey hand movements she realised that she was not going to get much, if any satisfaction, from the few male members of the audience.

Never mind.

She gave up on Facelift Freda sitting beside her and turned to the person on her other side.

"My goodness," exclaimed Wunderwear, "what fantastic hair."

The lower middle aged, well preserved and good looking woman next to her turned and smiled in a friendly manner. Her oval face was crowned by golden tresses, flowing around her shoulders and down her back.

"You like my hair then do you? Took me ages and cost a fortune to get it this way, the way I like it," the woman said her face glowing in response to Wunderwear's enthusiasm.

"Oh yes," enthused Wunderwear, "I'd love to have hair like that. In fact, look, I know it's a bit pushy, and you don't have to agree, but would you mind, really mind if I tried it on? Do you think it would fit and suit my style?"

The glow disappeared from the woman's face, she looked at Wunderwear with contempt and turned away.

"What a lot of miserable unsociable bitches," thought Wunderwear, "can't even hold a decent conversation. I bet they're all fur coat and no knickers."

She settled down to watch the show.

Thunderous, exciting, powerful music was followed by dismal, bored looking models prancing like dressage horses down the catwalk instead of walking. Yep the director definitely studied at the Monty Python Ministry of Funny Walks. What sort of twit makes them do that?

Wunderwear was puzzled. "Why didn't they look happy in their work? Were they uncomfortable in the clothes? Admittedly the clothes were crap and unwearable but at least they could try, couldn`t they?"

She looked at the women on either side of her but couldn't attract their attention. They had already had enough of her style of conversation.

She turned round and said to the flamboyantly dressed guy behind her, "excuse me but why do they look so miserable up there? They prance along in a trance, no character, no style, no nothing. Why?"

"Loooook darling," he cooed, flapping his hands like a limp lettuce, "it's not about them, it's about the clothes you see luvvy. They have to submerge their own characters. Everything should be hidden by the garments. They should only be judged by their clothes, they should not be seen as a person."

"Oh," said Wunderwear, "it's an Arab fashion show. Are they allowed to drive?"

The guy looked totally confused so Wunderwear faced the front.

Eventually and none too soon for Wunderwear all the models came on stage and politely tapped their dainty fingers together in what was supposed to be a clap. This was a sign for the designer to appear to huge waves of applause.

Every designer always had to appear in clothes that screamed out, "look darlings, I'm creative, I'm a designer you know." They always wore stuff that was a damn sight more fun than those worn by the models. Obviously saved the best for themselves. They loved themselves more than the women they tried to dress.

Wunderwear applauded wholeheartedly delighted that it was all over. She supposed that the others were doing it for the same reason.

As she turned to leave she bumped Facelift Freda with her backside plumping her back in her seat.

Wunderwear was full of concern, grabbed hold of her hands and pulled her up.

She looked hard at the woman, felt up and down her arms and said with great empathy, "my goodness, all that surgery and you missed out on your arms. You haven't just got chicken wings my dear, they're as big as a turkey's gizzard.

Still I suppose that they're too far gone really, aren't they? If you had this lot tucked up then your elbows would be hanging around your collar bones. Ha ha ha, you wouldn't need shoulder pads, would you?"

The woman opened her mouth several times but no sound came out.

Wunderwear shrugged, seemed disappointed that the woman was apparently ungrateful for the attention and pushed her way out.

She passed the woman with the hair which wasn't hers and heard her say to a companion, "that's her, that's the insulting pushy fatso, all bum and botox."

"Botox!" screamed Wunderwear, "botox! Why you shaggy cow, this is all me, go on feel it. Squeeze my tits, pinch my bum, kiss my lips, in fact kiss my arse. No plastics here girl, no injections either. If a man gets hold of me he gets hold of a real woman. If he gets hold of you it's like going to the supermarket—everything's stuffed in plastic bags."

Wunderwear left yet another woman open mouthed and silent.

When she rejoined her friends they asked her if she enjoyed it.

"Nah," she said, "nobody did. Miserable bloody lot!"

# Back on Track

Wunderwear Woman was not happy. She felt she had gone off the rails somewhere along the way.

What did she have to do with fashion shows and other worlds?

When she flounced in wearing a long skirt split up to the top of her thighs together with a transparent blouse open to her waist and no bra her friends threatened to emigrate.

When she asked them to accompany her to discover the Third World the same friends wanted to stay put.

"Look Wunderwear," one of them said, "you are trying too hard. There are the poor, dumb and disabled, right out there on the street, cardboard cities galore, right in front of your eyes. Enough to occupy you for years. Get on your bike and go and help them."

"Right, okay then," she thought, "tomorrow I get started. Good idea."

And the next day she did.

She went to the YMCA, The Salvation Army, a Christian hostel and the Samaritans.

She burst into a hostel full of enthusiasm. "Here I am, ready to go, what do want me to do?" she shouted gleefully.

"He gave misfortune a bad name!"

"Be quiet or bugger off," moaned an old dilapidated wreck in the corner trying to keep a reed thin cigarette from total collapse.

"Well that's not very Christian is it?" exclaimed Wunderwear.

"That's 'cos I bloody well ain't one am I?" answered the wreck.

"Well what you doing here then?" asked Wunderwear.

"Waiting to be chucked out 'en I, that's what," said Mr. Dilapidated.

"Oh," said Wunderwear, "you don't work here then?"

"Cause not, you barmy or sumthin', I don't work, do I?" he said, "I'm one of your long term unemployed enn I?"

"Are you?" said Wunderwear, in what she hoped was a sympathetic voice.

"Yep, unemployable, that's what I am," he said proudly, "I'm a victim of an unjust society, that's what I am."

"No you're not," said a soft voice from behind Wunderwear, "you're a lazy, conniving, dishonest old devil and you're taking up space that's needed by someone really deserving. On your way Mr. Hudson."

Mr. Hudson stood up, walked out, giving a finger as he went.

"Sorry about that. Can I help you?" The voice came from a stocky, comfortable, grey haired woman dressed in sensible clothes.

Wunderwear was a little put out. Wasn't that just the sort of person she had set out to save? Shouldn't someone be saving him?

She asked the woman that question.

"Mr. Hudson is not a victim but unfortunately everyone he comes into contact with soon becomes one. *He gives misfortune a bad name.* We are a shelter for the homeless and needy not a fertile breeding ground for a den of thieves. There are genuine people who really are victims of a very selfish, unjust and unequal society and we do our best to get them through a bad time. He's not one of them. The rumour is that he was a Butler once. What can we do for you?"

"I want to help" said Wunderwoman in an appealing voice, "I thought I could help you here."

"What qualifications and experience do you have," asked the woman in a no nonsense voice, "I'm Deirdre by the way."

"Well I'm nice," Wunderwear said, trying to sound convincing.

"Great, so was Jesus and he got himself crucified. What else can you do besides nice?" asked Deirdre.

"I can cook, wash dishes, clean and carry," said Wunderwear triumphantly, "is that nice enough for you?"

"You're in." laughed the woman, "you just got yourself a job. When can you start?"

"Right away, what do you pay?"

"We don't. We're volunteers."

"In that case I can start tomorrow, evenings only."

"Okay, can you be here by 5.30, that's when we open our doors for the evening? We lock our doors at 10 and finish up around midnight. See you tomorrow if you don`t change your mind." said Deirdre.

"My goodness, this being helpful stuff isn't easy," Wunderwear thought, "These people must be really good."

"Deirdre, dealing with some of the world's very human disasters."

When she arrived the next day at 5.30 she saw a long queue of people bunched up by the doors, stretching a long way back and round the nearest corner. They all looked downcast, dejected and humiliated. Smiles were few and laughter rare. They'd all done that in the past and got nowhere. They would leave that to the perfect white teeth crowd.

She made her way round the opposite corner and found a side door. She slipped in and found a hive of activity.

She was greeted with hellos and high fives and then ignored.

She asked the way to the kitchen, followed the direction of the nods and was immediately swept up in preparing food, sorting plates and preparing trestle tables for distribution.

The doors opened and the crowds piled in.

It was everyone for themselves. Their needs were simple, get food, get a bed and get cleaned up.

Some had jobs but were too lowly paid to be able to afford accommodation or basic amenities. Others had bad habits that reduced their ability to earn or save but most didn't. They couldn't afford any bad habits in the first place.

A number were bright enough but down on their luck while too many had not had any luck in the first place.

All the workers were compassionate but business like. They had seen so much for so long. A lot of them had returned from overseas overwhelmed by the poverty and suffering they had seen but were not beaten by it. They would work on irrespective.

After lights out the staff grouped together for a drink and chat. One or two maintained a night time vigil to cut down on any illegal activity. They were mostly successful.

They had to deal with incontinence, sickness, nightmares, theft, violence and pure bloodymindedness.

They did.

Wunderwear was curious.

"Why are you necessary?" she asked, "doesn't the government do anything?"

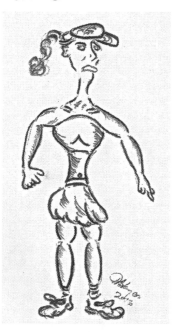

"Governments do some, but not much," said one tough wisp of a girl.

"Some but not much," said one tough wisp of a girl who appeared harassed and hectic most of the time.

"Why?"

"Because it's fashionable propaganda to have as little government as possible. It's convenient for the have's to be self righteous and blame the have nots for not having anything." said wispy girl.

"Learned economists, with tunnel vision, adhere to three hundred year old doctrines, sticking with the trickle down effect when what is needed is a damn great flood. Corporations who have amassed great fortunes invest in new equipment that puts out of work the very thousands who created the fortune in the first place. Then they send out the story that it`s the workers fault that they are unemployed. Of course sometimes it is but mainly it isn't. Good one that isn't it?" said an earnest professor type gent.

Learned Economists with tunnel vision sticking to 300 year old obsolete theories.

"Do you know that so many of the strongest opponents of government policies put forward to help the poor, sick and underprivileged call themselves Christians. So much for the teachings of gentle Jesus eh?" said wispy.

Wunderwear thought this was stunning and couldn't wait to get back to her friends on her day off. She was full of enthusiasm. They were in the White Collar Wine Bar as usual, needing a few stiffeners after a hard day sitting on their backsides in the office.

"Do you know that the world is full of silly, selfish, greedy, grab all people?" Wunderwear blurted out to a startled audience, "and we should take more care of the young, the old, the sick, the poor and the needy. We should share more."

"We should share and care more," exclaimed Wunderwear.

Oh my god, are you a socialist?" cried her friend
Naomi Overly-Pomp.

"Oh my god! Are you a socialist?" exclaimed her friend Naomi Overly-Pomp.

"Why, is that bad?" asked Wunderwear.

"Bad! Heavens! To people like us it's a dangerous disease," came the answer.

"Does it mean you're a socialist if you care" said Wunderwear plaintively.

"Don't be so pathetic and naive, of course caring doesn't make you a socialist, we all care, but if you actually do something about it then you turn into one of them, said Naomi scornfully.

"Don't become one of those bleeding heart specimens," interrupted Fiona Blind-Spot, "As if we could all share more. Why should I, or anyone else give anything away? Just pretend to care sweetie, like we all do."

"But doesn't that make us selfish hypocrites?" asked Wunderwear.

"Of course darling, that's why we're so successful," came the retort.

Wunderwear woman stuck it out for a few weeks, tried the YMCA and Salvation Army and found the same problems faced by the same group of dedicated people trying to introduce kindness into a harsh selfish world.

A short spell with the Samaritans she found to be the worst of all. Here they dealt with those who felt they had no hope at all. Desperate people who were reaching out to try to find a straw to cling to. Some were attention seeking time wasters but most were not.

Wunderwear woman started to wilt. This was not any Star Trek nor life as she knew it.

It was all too complicated. It appeared that Governments shirked their responsibility to parts of their own population because they were inconvenient, embarrassing and detrimental to their own re-election chances. They dumped the responsibility elsewhere onto good hearted people while allowing criticism of the aid given to those who they felt to be losers.

Wunderwear yearned to go back to her smug middle class friends and lose herself in admiration of the indifferent rich. Much more rewarding and much less depressing. She longed for a mind dumbing afternoon in the armchair looking at a couple of hours of 'E' on TV. Yep the Americans had evolved dumb and dumber into an art form.

She talked it over with Dierdre. This was deep stuff and Wunderwear said she wanted to save the whole world not just the lost and lonely parts of it.

Dierdre understood. She explained, "We and others look from the top down. The world looks a lot different from the bottom up. The have's always badly judge the have nots. It is easy from the top down because you have an escape clause. You can always leave the dirt and deprivation behind but from the bottom up you cannot. You are stuck there as well as having to put up with smug superiority, condemnation and patronisation from the have's.

"Yep," said Wunderwear, "I understand. With money life becomes simple for those who have it and tough for those who don't."

"Try telling an illegal immigrant escaping rape and murder in her own country, working 90 hours a week for a dollar a day that she doesn't work hard enough. Tell a starving child worker doing the same in the Third World that poverty is its own fault for not trying more," Deirdre said, "so you either empathise and help or dodge the issue by telling yourself and everyone that they don't deserve any help anyway."

Wunderwear thought, "Oh dear, I do think that. I bet they don't deserve it. They would probably only turn to drink and drugs. Just like the wealthy."

Yeah, there you go, she felt better already.

All she had needed was a dose of bourgeois therapy.

The wonderful USA was brilliant at marketing poverty as an asset. All you had to do be was a hardworking, patriotic 'All American' and you too could share the dream of being made in the USA. Everyone could be rich if they dreamed because Walt Disney said so.

Dreams are fine but eventually you have to wake up to reality.

Wunderwear suddenly did.

She needed to lose weight and get fit.

Then she could take on the world.

# Fit to Drop

Wunderwear enrolled at the local fitness centre. She refused the introductory tour as being a waste of energy. After all a girl only had so much to give.

She was so eager to get to it that she didn't bother about changing. Nobody would notice anyway as her normal daywear would pass for going anywhere other than a black tie affair.

She tossed a huge towel around her neck and tried to work on her entrance. She couldn't decide on whether to take an athletic bound through the doors or a furtive slink.

She practised for a while and decided that the bound was more positive.

She dived in, looked around and saw no one. The place was deserted.

"My god," she thought, "so much stuff and no humans."

There was row after row of running machines, cycling machines and no end of flat and inclined boards. There were contraptions so complex that Wunderwear got pulled muscles and dislocated joints just thinking about them.

What to do and where to start?

A healthy fit young man in track suit bottoms and cut away top appeared out of nowhere.

He took over.

He was much too zealous for Wunderwear's liking.

He wanted blood tests, urine tests, blood pressure readings, temperature control and pulse beats. She was exhausted before she even started. In fact she was exhausted before he even started.

"Skip the tests and cut to the chase," she told him curtly.

"But it's our company policy," he argued.

"Change it or I'll find myself accidentally falling on you," Wunderwear snarled.

"Okay, okay, let me introduce you to the equipment?" he stuttered.

"Holey moley, you're going to introduce me," cried Wunderwear, "I thought that I was coming to a bloody gym not a cocktail party. Get on with it Fit Man."

Fit Man shrugged his shoulders in resignation, got her started on the running machine, very slowly, then went to check on a bicycle appliance and came back.

Wunderwear was gasping and clutching the hand rails in desperation. She had spread her legs so that she was no longer on the treadmill but standing on the sides.

"Shut --------the bloody ---------- thing ---------off, shut it off, shut it off," she panted, "I've got -------------- to get off."

"You are off, you're not on," said Fit Man, "get back on and I'll shut it off."

He was trying to be helpful by getting her to slide into the activity.

"To dream the Impossible Dream."

"Are you out of your stupid mind," screamed Wunderwear, "if I could stay on it I wouldn't be like this, would I? I couldn't keep up going forwards and kept on going backwards. I managed to grab hold of something and been like this until you came. So shut the fucking thing off now!"

He did. He wanted to point out that the controls were right in front of her on the panel but wisely decided not to.

Wunderwear gratefully collapsed but not before giving him a malevolent look.

After a long recovery period he helped her to the bike. He explained that she would like this as she would be sitting down.

She looked at him archly and with disdain.

"Look here Mr. Halfpint, I've been riding bikes since I was a little kid and they were the one's that moved. This one stays in one place I hope, so just let me at it if you don't mind. Lower the saddle please, how do you expect me to get my leg over? On second thoughts don't answer that. I'll manage."

She didn't. It took three people to separate her from the wreck of the machine. She was unhurt but very flustered.

The staff weren't in the least bit flustered, they were terrified.

What could they do? She was a member after all.

Trying to touch her toes was an impossible dream.

They tried to get her to jump up and down lifting her arms at the same time but she could only manage three or four at the most. They tried to encourage her but she told them to do it themselves.

They did—easily.

"Right," she said, "now do it lifting 250 lbs, 'cos that's what I'm doing."

They gave up and refunded her membership.

However Wunderwear found she still had the urge to do something to change her shape. She wanted to be remoulded.

One of her friends told her about a TV show that issued a challenge to heavyweights who wanted to be lightweights.

She watched it.

It was called a reality show but anything less real couldn't be imagined. As far as Wunderwear was concerned it appeared to feature overweight unhappy people with sado-machistic tendencies who didn't mind being abused and humiliated in public by insecure bullies who couldn't tear their eyes away from the camera.

She liked it.

She applied but was rejected. During the tests she took things very personally and flattened two instructors who when they eventually recovered decided to work elsewhere. One producer thought that she would be a big draw but changed her mind when Wunderwear rejected her sexual advances.

Wunderwear once again had to reassess her life.

# Holiday Times

Wunderwear decided she needed to get away. She was suffering from "Lack of Holiday Blues."

So why not go to the home of the Blues. The Blues were born in the USA along with much else. So the USA it was.

It was Winter in the UK so she decided to go to Florida, the Sunshine State.

She flew business class to Miami. She loved business class because of all the space. Airlines never marketed it in that way. They always showed those synthetic, slim, far too beautiful smarmy people posing and getting settled and serviced. They never considered magnificent people like Wunderwear Woman as being their target audience.

"Stuff them, that's their loss," thought Wunderwear.

She checked into her hotel on Miami Beach, with a sea facing room. The other rooms looked back across the Intra-Coastal to the mainland.

She realised she needed feeding.

"Yeah," she said to herself, "America's lousy on quality but great on quantity, especially ketchup and mayonnaise. Let me at it."

She took a cab, telling the driver she was a gourmet that needed a big meal. He didn't get the gourmet part but understood big.

"Grande, si?"

"You got it, go Mex go," she cried enthusiastically.

He shook his head at the Mex bit, and doubled the fare.

Wunderwear realised they were going off the Beach onto the mainland and heading downtown.

They kept going and she started to get nervous.

Was she being abducted, would she be raped, tortured and murdered?

The rape bit she could cope with but didn't fancy the torture and murder scenario at all. It was all very well having bad experiences. You could recover from them, they were all part of life, but she couldn't remember anyone having recovered from murder especially if pain was inflicted first.

"Nope," she thought, "don't fancy that. I will give this guy a few more minutes and then I'm going to bash him one, take over the cab and go back to town."

The driver looked at her in the mirror, smiled and said, "you are in for a treat tonight lady, Mex style. We're into the Everglades. I gotta great place in mind. Be careful when you get out though, the crocs may be hungry."

"Oh my god, he's going to rape me and then feed me to the crocs," she cried inwardly, "there's so much of me I'll keep 'em occupied for days and there's no one here to miss me."

They swung into a short drive, flooded with lights and stopped in front of a windowless building. Bright neon signs flickered above double batwing doors saying Mex Max.

The driver grinned, "you said 'go Mex go' so we've gone. Enjoy, lady enjoy."

She paid off the cabbie who gave her his card and said, "call me when you're ready to go."

"What," she exclaimed, "we're miles out of town. I'll be waiting here half the night for you to come back. Are you nuts?"

"Nope, I'm gonna grab a sandwich and catch up on my sleep right here in the parking lot. I caught the nightshift this week," he said, "take your time."

As soon as Wunderwear entered the restaurant she loved it.

"Wow, this is a country that knows how to feed people. Gluttony is in!"

"Wow," she exclaimed, "oh yeah, all the women look like me, in fact they make me feel small. I love 'em. This is a country that knows how to feed people. Gluttony is in! Sit me down and get me started."

A waitress came over managing to look smart and slovenly at the same time.

Wunderwear felt it to be a peculiarity of the States that they never really managed to get it together. Those who dressed well behaved badly and those who dressed badly behaved better. Those who had money looked cheap and those who were poor looked worse. But everyone was always so positive. Whatever.

Except for waitresses.

This one had a disinterested expression on her face as she said, "hi, how yere doing?"

She didn't wait for a reply as she launched into dozens of options and promotions. Wunderwear wondered when she would get to the ordering and eating bit, so she tried to interrupt. At first she was ignored, the robot carried on reciting, so she persisted, finally making a breakthrough. She felt as though she had pulled a plug.

The waitress looked puzzled and concerned.

"Ah bayg yah pardon," she drawled, "do ya awl wanna order now?"

Wunderwear turned around. Yes, she was on her own, who else was the woman talking to? "No, not yet. Could you repeat that part about the red snapper please?"

"What part?"

"How do I know, you were doing the telling. If I knew I wouldn't have to ask would I?" Wunderwear asked in a reasonable tone.

The waitress was puzzled, she always just recited what she had been told at the pre-opening briefing, no one had instructed her on how to answer probing questions.

So she started at the beginning again with an expression on her face that prohibited further questions.

Wunderwear switched off and studied the menu.

The waitress finished and looked expectantly at Wunderwear.

Wunderwear kept it simple. Medium cooked steak and fries with side salad and French dressing. The waitress seemed about to launch into a further discussion but changed her mind, turned and disappeared in the direction of the kitchen.

"Phew," thought Wunderwear, "what a performance. Takes so long. How on earth do they get so big? Wait a minute, perhaps that's why. It takes so long to order that they are starving by the time the food comes. So they over compensate. Yeah that must be it."

The food arrived. Salad first.

Wunderwear wanted it to come together with the steak.

The waitress raised her eyebrows at this as though to say, "foreigners!" but she complied.

Wunderwear thought that of all places the USA was not in any position to complain about foreigners. They were all foreigners who had taken advantage of the wide open spaces and occupied the lands that the British, French and Spanish had colonised. All of them ignored the rights of the poor bloody Indians. They should learn how to behave.

When the steak came she couldn't help but utter a gasp. One gasp was not enough. She uttered two more.

The steak was impossibly huge. In the UK there would be enough to feed a family of four and leave enough for a stew the next day. The fries were piled as high as the pyramids. There was little sauce on the plate but enough bottles on the table to flood the place.

Wunderwear was content.

While chewing away she noticed a family standing close by. They were standing because they couldn't sit.

They stood no chance at all of sliding into the benches that were fixed to the tables. The space was generous enough, Wunderwear fitted okay, but this family group did not.

The guy was huge, but was dwarfed by his wife. The two children, a boy and a girl, although barely into their teens stood no chance of fitting in either.

The staff took it all in their stride. They pointed to a table fitted along the back wall. There was no fixed bench.

Stools were pulled out from underneath and the family sat down with more of their bellies and backsides hanging off the stools than actually fitted on them.

"I like it here," she said to herself, "even the small ones make me feel slim. I might consider staying a little longer."

Back at the hotel she checked with the hall porter about any activities and excursions but there were none that really suited her. The porter thought that there was more going on in Orlando.

Okay, she would go there later on she told him.

In the meantime she asked him where she could see some slim people and those heroic types that were in the movies. "You know," she said, "those hard bodied women, the rangy cowboys and them there manly do it all marines?"

"Lady," he laughed, "you won't see many around here. The only thin ones are the old gals who have had lippo suction, tummy tucks and yards of plastic surgery. You can recognise them by their jewellery and designer clothes that are meant for young bodies that can`t afford them. If you want slimmer, younger more glamorous women then you gotta go to New York. Them business types keep 'emselves smart. Have a nice day."

Wunderwear put Orlando and New York on her places to visit.

Wunderwear turned away.

"Just a minute, mam," the hall porter called after her, "I can understand a fine lady like you don't want to go diving, water skiing, or take a drunken boat trip, but how about deep sea fishing? You'd love it. Beers, barbecue and excitement, all in one.

Wunderwear thought about it, "Why not? Okay book me in."

She was ready, bright and early the next morning, waiting for the pickup truck.

It was on time.

She was taken to a great fishing boat, powerful and fast with a high turret built above the wheelhouse for a lookout.

She was introduced to the captain who was an older rugged guy, handsome, tanned and tough.

She was the only customer. Unusual but business had been slow so the captain had thought, "what the hell."

He had one helper who was the instructor, head cook and bottle washer all in one.

They set off, straight out to sea.

About an hour and several beers later the captain throttled back, handed over the deck to the assistant and took control from the tower.

He was content to poodle around until he saw what he was looking for.

There a half mile away was a pile of driftwood, seaweed and rubbish. They headed straight for it and stopped just short.

The captain explained that in the heat of mid morning the fish looked for shade. There would be some tucked underneath the pile out there but how many and how big was not obvious. The only way to find out was to put out the lines and do a fast pass.

It was necessary to go fast because that way the big fish would chase and maybe bite. A slow pass would allow smaller fish to catch on.

They set off with the assistant watching the rods intently.

Suddenly one started twitching. Wunderwear was bundled swiftly into a revolving chair, strapped in and the base of the rod slipped into a harness that had been strapped onto her. Her hands were wrapped tightly around the rod and the instructions came thick and fast.

The fish would soon catch on that it was caught and would start to fight. The bigger the fish the stronger and longer would be the fight. The trick was to reel it in close enough to be netted and not let it off the hook.

Wunderwear was shown how to lower the rod to give a bit of slack and then suddenly pull it back up, then lower it again at the same time reeling in fast.

Wow, the power of the fish suddenly became very obvious. Several times the rod was nearly torn out of her hands but she hung on grimly, steadily reeling in. The fish got up to all sorts of tricks. It would run in fast and then dive or it would attempt to run under the keel hoping to sever the line. The captain was alert all the time, running away when it dived, turning sharply when it went under the keel or reversing if the fish tried to go in the opposite direction trying to stretch rod and reel beyond their limits.

Wunderwear had no idea it could be so absorbing and exciting. This was more basic and natural than going out on a big trawler and scooping everything up in a net. She felt heroic and primitive.

"Yeah Mister Ernest Hemingway, eat your heart out, now I know what it's all about," she shouted.

This was one fish that was well and truly hooked. They eventually landed it in the boat. It was a huge Yahoo. They also caught some Snappers and a Dory but a Tuna escaped much to the chagrin of the captain.

Their activity had attracted the attention of other boats. The area was becoming crowded, so they pronounced themselves satisfied with the catch and headed home.

Wunderwear learned that the catch traditionally belonged to the skipper but a large Snapper was given to her as a prize.

A bigger prize was in store for her.

The assistant took charge of the run in while the captain relaxed with Wunderwear and a few beers.

He suggested that they sit under the canopy at the rear so as to be out of the sun.

Wunderwear agreed.

"This is the life," she said to the skipper, "better than sex."

"What!" exclaimed the captain, "what the hell you been doing? Nothing's better than sex. You crazy or something?"

"Nope," said Wunderwear quietly, "not crazy, just frustrated, that's all."

"Look, nobody's frustrated on my boat, ain't allowed, so get yourself on over here," the captain said with a big grin.

"Naaaaaah, you don't mean it," said Wunderwear a bit sheepishly, "I wish you did though."

"Okay, you won't come to me then I'll come to you because I sure do mean it." the captain said as he slid along the padded seat.

He cupped Wunderwear's face in his two hands and kissed her full on the mouth complete with tongue.

As he pulled back Wunderwear grabbed him. She wasn't going to let this pass her by.

She was trying to undo his shirt and trousers, kiss and caress him all at the same time. She succeeded with the loss of only a few buttons.

Her leotard and bicycle shorts were more of a problem but even though she was so excited she still managed to slip out of them pretty smartly.

They were both panting in their underwear. He was in boxer shorts with a rampant dick clearly trying to push its way out while she was in knickers and bra longing for it to be pushed in. She struggled with his boxers and he struggled with her bra. They both made it at the same time and both gasped in delight. She couldn't believe the size of his rock hard cock and he couldn't believe the shape and firmness of her magnificent great boobs.

She slid both her hands round his prick and stroked it lovingly. "Oh boy, do I love fishing," she laughed. He had pulled down her pants and she kicked them off.

He started gentle foreplay but Wunderwear was too far gone.

"No, don't muck about, I want you in me, now, now now, oh please, please now," she cried as she laid herself out obligingly along the seat, "I have had years of touch ups, I do it to myself all the time, so go deep inside me, I'm ready."

And she was.

He took her front, back and sides. She came time and time again, she didn't know how many times because she wasn't counting.

The captain told the crewman to take the boat in and out again several times. They went in and out again many times before they both collapsed satisfied.

Wunderwear felt a little awkward and embarrassed as she dressed knowing his eyes were on her.

"It's incredible," she thought, "that you're never embarrassed as your clothes come off, only when they go back on. Seems to be the wrong way round really."

She looked shyly across at him. He was still naked and made no move to dress.

He was watching her.

Wunderwear became conscious of her body. Should she be ashamed? Dammit no, maybe her size was a health hazard but it was her health and her hazard so she straightened her back, stretched up and looked confident.

Within seconds she was on her back again, thrusting her butt up as he thrust down and in.

"Wow," she gasped, "what happened there?"

"You happened," he said, "if you want to get off this boat tonight then you'd better not do that again."

She didn't want to get off the boat so she did do it again.

She hadn't realised how much she had missed the sex bit. This wasn't love, it was pure lust and it was wonderful. She was a straightforward girl who preferred the great love affair, monogamy and family but in the absence of that ultimate package then this would do very nicely thank you.

She knew all the old clichés and had lived most of them but the one about hating yourself the next morning was not going to apply here. She would love and hug herself for days.

She finally staggered back to the hotel at dawn with a very satisfied, smug look on her face.

What a trip. What a catch.

The hotel kitchen served up the fish on a silver platter cooked in a wonderful sauce.

She knew exactly what it felt like.

She was also wise enough not to go back the next day.

She'd seen the movie "Shirley Valentine."

The captain always caught fresh fish. He had no interest in the previous day's catch or leftovers and neither had Wunderwear.

Time to move on.

"The day's catch served up on a plate."

Before she left she decided to do a little shopping. She topped up on snacks in the nearby supermarket. While in the queue to pay she was held up as the old lady in front was dithering a bit. The check out girl showed her impatience. The old woman looked up, looked hard at the girl and said in a wonderful relaxed southern drawl, "young lady you are so rude. You must be from New York."

She was!

As she was leaving the shop the staff burst out laughing at something a DJ had just said on the local radio station. She asked what it was.

"Folks, today should be fine all day, blue skies, bright sun and calm seas. That's good news but it get's even better. Hundreds of tourists have been seen heading back up north. Can anything be better than that? Yes it can. They were all Canadian!"

She went to Orlando but found that she didn't need Disney or the Water Parks but Epcot and the NASA Space Center were fantastic.

She drooled over them.

In Epcot she travelled through primeval forests spooked by dinosaurs, flew space missions and took a peep into the future. She couldn't believe how everything rolled from briefing through to virtual reality without a hitch.

NASA was breathtaking.

She relived an entire spaceflight launch and control and roamed around acres of actual disused hardware. The real life size of everything was staggering.

The thought of Disney compelled her to take a look. She was most impressed with the efficient way they handled hundreds of people at a time at the entrance but found that she had long outgrown Snow White and Mickey Mouse. Bambi and Dumbo were great though.

Then she found International Studios.

Real life movies.

She took part in disasters and saw the recovery which was novel for her as she often caused similar chaos with little recovery. She walked through movie lots that she recognised and acted out a few parts until she became aware of some others looking at her strangely. Some people huh!

Then the finale was a whole scene from a famous action movie which was so real that it was startling.

She decided that she needed to review all her opinions on movies and actors as they really did create miracles of deception.

Magic, real magic.

Where next she thought.

Two weeks were soon going to be used up.

It had to be New York.

She was on her way.

# The Big Apple

Kennedy Airport was at full capacity so Wunderwear landed at Newark in New Jersey.

This meant a view of the Statue of Liberty and Manhattan from the other side and a ride through the tunnel.

Great.

The skyline had changed of course. No more World Trade Buildings.

Wunderwear loved to read the so called conspiracy theorists who believed that everyman and his dog had destroyed them except for those who actually did do it.

She believed that it said more about the deranged minds of the theorists than it did about the terrible event. The Nazis proved that if you can keep on repeating the same lies then some idiots will believe them. Some still do!

The taxi had to take her uptown to the Sheraton on 6th Avenue, close to Carnegie Hall and most importantly the Stage Deli.

She checked in first and then went out for a walk.

My god, so many copies of everything laid out on the pavement by illegal immigrants galore.

She asked one of the guys if they were copies just to make sure. He didn't know much English but appeared hurt by the question. No they weren't copies, they were real copies.

She thought that the USA was the main protector of Copyrights but apparently only at long distance. Closer to home they were apparently very shortsighted!

Twice she was accosted by men of complex ethnic origin who when she refused to respond got shirty and said, "hey, respect me man. Give me some respect."

"Okay," said Wunderwear, "you got my respect, now leave me alone and respect me and my privacy. Bye, see you."

"Bloody hell," she thought, "friendliness is one thing but pushy is another. What is going on?"

She had been headed downtown but decided to reverse and went back towards Central Park.

She had to get used to the pedestrian cross signs at junctions. She wanted to rush across at any break in the traffic but soon learned it was not allowed. She realised that after suffering considerable abuse from drivers.

Luckily she escaped the attention of the police.

She learned patience only to find that it didn't pay off because instead of a traffic build up there was a pedestrian backlog and if she didn't barge on then she got left behind.

That was without trying to duck and dive to avoid those coming in a hurry from the other side.

She didn't like crossing roads at all in this city but it was unavoidable due to the monotonous squared layout. Travel one block, wait, then cross to another block, wait, then cross, and so it went on forever. The locals seemed to find this fascinating and navigated by it.

Boring. But Central Park wasn't.

She took a leisurely ride in a carriage. De luxe version.

She relaxed, took in all she needed to see and chatted to the coachman.

He told her that the business was a good investment if the weather held, and he had had to buy the concession in the first place. The same applied to hotel doormen's jobs in the city. Basically you had to buy the other guy out.

So much for fair, open competition based on suitability and capability. Cronyism was in!

She roamed around, saw some art, visited some museums, looked up at buildings, rejected Trump as typical nouveau riche bling bling. Didn't anyone tell him it was New York, not Las Vegas? She tried to look at the people which should have been easy but wasn't. They never stood still for a second unless at intersections but even there they managed to look in a hurry when not even moving.

Stage Deli she loved. Boy oh boy could they make a sandwich. She favoured pastrami on rye with two pickles. While there she was witness to typical New York enterprise.

A guy was sitting in the corner nursing a cup of coffee well away from the door. The proprietor came around the counter, went over to him and said, "Excuse me, what do ya think this place is, a waiting room or something?

This ain't a big place, I gotta turn these tables over a dozen times a day and I can't do that if you take root. Now you gotta buy something or go, okay?"

The guy went without leaving a tip followed by a sardonic, "thank you," from the boss.

Wunderwear decided not to sit down for long. Keep moving was obviously the trend there.

The Empire State Building was back in fashion. It was never going to regain its old status as the icon of NY but it still gave a bird's eye view of the city. With a little effort you could imagine King Kong holding Faye Wray adoringly in the palm of his huge hand while clinging onto the building and swatting away at the attacking paper and wood aeroplanes. No mean feat. Wunderwear wondered if she would ever have someone love her like that. She was a lot more substantial than Faye Wray.

A big Ape would do nicely.

That reminded her of the guys down her local pub.

It was time to go home.

# Straight Sex

Wunderwear was home. She couldn't wait to tell her friends of her holiday adventures.

She cornered them at Diva's Deli and Wine Emporium just when they'd reached the 'oh my god' and 'awesome' stage after the 'cool' period but before they started jumping up and down with shrieks and false screams of surprise.

They weren't very impressed with most of the events but when Wunderwear got to the fishing trip they edged forward hanging on every word of the seduction.

Fiona Blind-Spot was wriggling around like a worm trying to dig a hole in concrete. "Darling, do tell, give us every detail, did you experiment at all," she managed to utter breathlessly, "like, I mean did you get on top or anything, how many pushes did he manage before the explosion, did you have an orgasm?"

"Don't be daft," exclaimed Naomi Overly-Pomp, "she doesn't know what that is, do you sweetie?"

"Do you mean did he last longer than the five minute selfish wonders who fuck you and roll off knackered before you`ve even begun to get underway?

Do you mean did I come and come again and again because of all the things he was doing to me, some at the same time?

Do you mean did I eat him and did he eat me. Did I scream, did I shout, did I want and get more?

The answer is YES, YES YES and OH YES!!" she shouted.

The Deli been silent for a while and Wunderwear was loud. It seemed that everyone had shared her experience.

Her friends were stunned.

There was a round of applause from the crowd and Fiona asked quietly, "Where was it you went fishing?"

Naomi however was shocked. Not because she was embarrassed by Wunderwear's ecstatic revelations but because she became aware for the first time that she may have missed something by being so selective down the gym.

Wunderwear told her, "you realise that we nearly always choose those pumped up pinheads who are so full of themselves they can't fill us. They fasten onto us frustrated women. We're so grateful to get anything that we hunger for more because what we do get is very little actually.

I tell you gal that once you've had it the way I've had it you won't want those selfish sods anymore. Look at some of 'em here. They lust and leer after us, telling each other what they'd do if they got the chance, yet most of 'em are out of breath walking to the bar.

Those who can still breathe can't stop posing and pissing.

Get a fit modest older man. Don't waste yourself on a young show off. They're all wannabees. Go and get a bit of the real thing, luvvie, in fact go get a lot!!"

"I get quite a bit you know," said a woman leaning over from the next table. Wunderwear took a quick look, a little puzzled at the intrusion but it was Naomi who interjected eagerly with, "oh really, do tell."

"Down girl," laughed Wunderwear at Naomi, "take a good look."

She then turned to the woman saying, "not being rude lady but I've seen myself in the mirror and I go begging but compared to you I'm Helen of Troy.

She launched a thousand ships and you'd sink 'em. We're not interested in fantasies just now, we've had enough of them. I've had a touch of reality. I've had a real man. That's what I'm talking about."

"Whose talking men?" said the woman evenly. "Who needs those beasts when we have ourselves?"

"Yeah, right on," giggled Fiona, "When I get really heated up I have a bit of myself all right, unless I can find a carrot of course. Nothing like an organic orgasm."

She shrugged at all the raised eyebrows. "Well I like it anyway," she said rather too defensively.

"Nothing like an organic orgasm. Well I like it anyway," she said defensively.

"I have my partner, Aileen, she's here, getting the drinks in," said the woman, ignoring all the remarks, "this is her now."

Wunderwear and friends looked up.

"Right, got it now," exclaimed Wunderwear shortly, "yup, you're a pair of lezzies right, so enjoy your beers and we'll carry on talking."

"You're not homophobic are you," asked the woman as her partner was sitting down passing her a beer across the table.

"Only when you drink beer in a wine bar and interrupt our conversation" said Naomi very primly, "just because you're butch you don't have to overdo it you know."

"I don't think this is a good idea Shauna," said Aileen, "this lot are not going to understand."

"Oi you, short back and sides and Doc Martins," cried Wunderwear, "we are not this lot, we are us, you know, normal like? We understand. Your pal 'ere is after converts and we're not in for it."

"I'm afraid I've upset you and that wasn't my intention," said Shauna a bit on the weepy side.

"See what you've done," said Aileen harshly, "she's upset now. She's so sweet you know. She's too good to be in this world."

"Oh I'm sorry," said Fiona putting her arm around Shauna's shoulder and giving her a hug.

"Get off her," shouted Aileen, "she's not a slut you know. She's mine. She's not like you putting yourselves around cheaply everywhere."

She pulled Shauna away rather roughly saying, "for crissakes I can't leave you for five minutes without you coming on to somebody."

"Thought she was sweet and too good for this world," mumbled Wunderwear, "What's going on here girls?"

They had attracted the attention of Philip, one of the barmen. "No problem I hope, I don't want any flying handbags tonight," he said with an ingratiating smile.

"Don't worry," said Wunderwear, "these two aren't into handbags. Socks with sand in are more their type. No need to get your old boxer shorts into a twist."

Her friends snickered.

Philip looked uncertain, seemingly in two minds but said, "okay, just keep it down, alright?"

Naomi was puzzled, "how do you know he wears old boxers?"

"Yeah," exclaimed Fiona "how?"

"Oh my god, he's had us all then, hasn't he?" laughed Wunderwear, "I bet they're his seduction shorts. He didn't wear the Union Jack one's for you as well did he?"

"No, it was the Stars and Stripes for me," shrieked Naomi.

"I got the Star of David," roared Fiona.

"I bet you did," cried Wunderwear.

They all collapsed with laughter.

"Pathetic, absolutely pathetic," said Aileen, "tell 'em Shauna."

Wunderwear and friends had completely forgotten the intruders.

"You can only find true love with a woman. Only a woman understands what another woman wants," Shauna said sweetly, while Aileen smiled rather patronisingly.

"I'm glad of that," said Wunderwear smartly, "got it in one. Aileen is really a bloke right?"

"No," said Shauna bewildered, "Aileen is a woman."

"Well then, Shauna, sorry but she hasn't got what we want then. Love it and hate it, for better or worse, we want a man. A man with the real thing between his legs and the means to use it. We don't want substitutes, or excuses or platitudes and in the end we want kids. Our kids, not someone else's. You do your thing and we'll do ours but don't come on with all those daft excuses for doing what you do," said Wunderwear triumphantly.

"Yeah you tell them girl," laughed Fiona, "we don't always get what we want but we know what we want and what the difference is when we get it. Well sometimes anyway. We are glorious women and proud of it."

"So Aileen and Shauna let's drink up to what we are, knock 'em back and get more in. Whoops! I mean the the drinks of course."

"I get more in, I get plenty," came a voice from behind, "drinks and a bit of the other."

"Bloody hell," exclaimed Wunderwear, "where did that come from? Is there no privacy here for crissakes?"

She looked around. Stood up. Looked again.

All she could see was an old couple sitting close by nursing two pints of Guinness.

"Nah, surely not them!" she thought.

"I tell you luv, we've been married 40 years and we've never stopped. Still go at it like a couple of rabbits, don't we Bert?" said the woman.

"More like Bonobos luv," said Bert, "we know all about Bonobos don't we Ada, seen 'em on Animal Planet, 'aven't we? Blimey they're at it all the time.

Makes us look a bit on the slow side and bloody hell we don't half give it a go."

Wunderwear's group were stunned and silent.

"Of course Ada ain't what she used to be, she could keep me going all night if she felt like it."

"Oh I felt like it," giggled Ada, "of course I didn't look like this, a real smasher I was and no mistake."

"Yeah a real sexy beauty," laughed Bert, "what I do now is close my eyes and try to remember."

"Oi, you saucy bugger," shouted Ada, "you're no Prince Charming to look at are you? I think of Gorgeous George, you know that Cloned fella."

"Clooney dear, Clooney," Bert corrected.

Fiona found her voice and asked in her fruity accent, "Excuse me for butting in but do I assume you are talking about sexual intercourse and not incontinence?"

"No luv, none of that fancy stuff. We're talking about a good old shag," Ada said.

"I guess you've lasted so long because you've both got your own space haven't you?" asked Naomi, trying hard to look serious and intelligent.

"No Ducky, we've not got our own space, we've got a ground floor maisonette, small but cosy. We rent it from the Council. It's alright though!" exclaimed Ada.

"I didn't mean that type of space, I meant personal space," Naomi said tartly.

"No luv, we're married. Marriage is shared space, there's two of you, you know. We had our own jobs but if you want your own space then don't agree to share your life. A shared life means a shared space," said Bert.

"If you're at work all day, get a few hours free in the evening if you're lucky and then sleep all night then you haven't got much time together have you? If you are moaning that you want more time on your own then you should just bugger off because you haven't got much of a marriage. You can have all the time and space in the world on your own but in marriage you have a partner. We've been together for ever. The only time we go anywhere different is when we go to the loo."

"He'd even go there if I let 'im," Ada giggled.

"Wow" cried Wunderwear, "you mean that you've only had each other and nobody else?"

"Don't be daft dear, I tried the rest and stuck with the best," Ada said quietly and smugly.

"What! what has Bert got to say about that?" asked Wunderwear.

"He's a bit deaf dear and always turned a blind eye," grinned Ada.

Bert studied his beer intently, then slowly lifted his head, looked at Wunderwear with a saucy expression on his face and winked.

"She still works you know," he said.

"Wow, at her age? What does she do?" asked Fiona.

"She's a porno star, you know that?" Bert said in all seriousness.

Everyone burst out laughing. "No, I mean it, she can turn on this delicious, lowdown sexy voice. She works for a Porno phone-in chat-line. She's Erotic Erica who strokes her pet python while you stroke yours! Great aren't you love?" Bert said proudly, "earns a bomb working nights she does."

"Yeah, I don't really listen to all the rubbish. Just breath heavy now and again and say 'ooooooooh, you are really turning me on now.' or 'you're such a naughty man, you've got my hands doing all sorts of things like crazy, what are you doing with yours or I'm so excited and shivering with delight' and then go back to my knitting. Nearly finished a nice fair isle pullover for Bert the other night," she said earnestly, "I'm a social worker performing a public service for all those poor mugs who can't get it up."

"Now I know where my community tax money goes," laughed Naomi, "you'll be telling me that they can get it on the National Health next."

"Too true love. We've got a few trustees on our books and I bet the authority pays their phone bills. Legitimate expenses my eye dearie. We're great for those who've got religion bad though. They can let loose their frustrations in private without whipping their backs and sticking nails in their thighs. Saves a lot of tears in their eyes. We always put a quid or two in the church collection box, don't we Bert?"

"Yeah. I phoned up once as a joke but she spotted me straight away and told me not to be such a silly sod and to get off the line."

"Nearly got me the sack as the supervisor told me she didn't give a bollocks who it was. Never turn away good money," Ada laughed.

"It was worth it though 'cos when she came home she gave me a right seeing to. Showed me we didn't need to fantasise, we could live it. Nothing like the real thing." said Bert, glowing at the memory.

Wunderwear and friends left feeling totally deflated and deprived.

"A shared life means a shared space."

# Diet

Wunderwear thought about dieting. She thought about it often but just as often rejected the idea.

The concept of fitting in to everything more easily had it's appeal of course but the thin ones always looked more miserable and intense than the chubby ones. A round face seemed happy and carefree with full lips and chubby cheeks whereas a thin face usually appeared worried and stressed.

Why suffer hunger pains just to look unhappy. Enjoy a good hearty meal for a change.

Along with a few friends she consulted a well recommended dietician, an expert no less from a local University. The learned professor's idea of advice came in the form of a lecture. At the end she asked if there were any questions.

"Yes," said Wunderwear, "I've got a few actually."

"Okay," said the prof' eagerly, "this is great, go ahead."

"Well you said we should avoid eating late in the evening because this would turn to unused fat as we go to sleep soon afterwards, right?"

"Yes, oh yes, go on," exclaimed the prof', "you really have been listening haven't you?"

"So why don't we do that to the starving people in say Ethiopia?" asked Wunderwear.

"Do what?" asked the prof' a little mystified.

96

"They all get a bit to eat, don't they, even though they're starving right? So why not give it to 'em late at night and they'll get fat and not be hungry, see what I mean? Simple ennit, problem solved?"

The professor initially seemed bemused but recovered and said, "right, well, what's another question then?"

"I don't see how there can be anyone starving in Africa anyway," declared Wunderwear, "they're all dead aren't they?"

"Are they, I didn't know?" said a now thoroughly confused lady.

"Yes, it's obvious isn't it? Wunderwear stated firmly, "I added up all the claims of the charities, organisations and governments the other day and found that 110% of Africans were either dead, dying or suffering from Aids, Malaria, Yellow Fever, starvation and goodness knows what else. Millions of them, can't be anyone left alive to feed. Don't know why anyone's worried about them being hungry. Just look up the statistics, Africans all gone, and we can go home."

Wunderwear smiled benignly.

"Do you have any actual questions about diet?" asked the professor a bit impatiently.

"Oh yeah," said Wunderwear, "of course,"

The professor winced before saying, "okay, go ahead."

"It's all very well saying eat this but don't eat that, right?"

"Right," said the professor hesitantly.

"But in fact we can't eat anything at all can we?" said Wunderwear.

"Why not?" asked the prof'.

"Because we're always getting red alerts, you know, warnings." said Wunderwear.

"The cows have mad cow disease, sheep have foot rot, chickens have bird flu' and eggs have salmonella. Don't leave much does it when fish are full of mercury and plants are sprayed with poison?"

"Apparently all foods in some way are bad for you and eating is dangerous. I can tell you now girl that starving is a bloody sight more dangerous. Now what's this diet you're recommending?"

"Maybe it won't suit you, it doesn't suit everyone you know," said the professor as she picked up her papers and left in a hurry.

"Well she wasn't very convincing was she?" Wundwerwear said to her friends, "asked for questions, didn't answer one of them and beat it without a word of goodbye. Never did think much of intellectuals, clever maybe but no commonsense. They'd believe anything."

Her friends looked about to say a lot but decided to keep quiet.

"You really have been listening, haven't you?"

# A Woman in Love

Wunderwear's friends were concerned. Since her return from the States she had been unsettled. She was far too critical of the men she met and came over all dreamy when anyone mentioned fishing.

They decided to open up their circle of friends. Naomi and Fiona hadn't been doing too well either so thought they could benefit as well.

Naomi favoured Facebook and Fiona liked Twitter.

Wunderwear thought that Twitter suited Fiona perfectly especially if she shortened it to Twit.

Naomi scored immediately on Facebook.

She was excited. She arranged a meet.

She'd tried before but the one's she met in real life didn't match up to their Facebook resume.

She was gushing, "he's gorgeous, absolutely gorgeous."

"Come on, if he's that gorgeous, he's gay," laughed Fiona.

"He's not," exclaimed Naomi indignantly.

"Why have you tried it yet?" asked Wunderwear.

"No, not exactly, but I've felt it, Naomi said rather petulantly.

Fiona giggled, "So okay, he's got one but how do you know exactly where he puts it?"

"Well I don't yet do I? I'm not that cheap and easy like some," she said pointedly, looking straight at Wunderwear.

"Don't look at me, the chance would be great," complained Wunderwear, going all dreamy again. "anyway you didn't get the nickname 'Lucy Lastic' because you were slow in getting them off did you?"

"Come on girls, don't let's fight, let's enjoy. When do we meet him?" said Fiona.

"Tonight. He's coming to the Wine Bar, and, and, wait for it, he's bringing a friend," Naomi revealed a little too breathlessly.

"What," shrieked Wunderwear and Fiona together, "my god, what will we wear?"

Both friends looked at Wunderwear in amazement. Fiona of course would come looking like some frail Dresden Doll dressed in Laura Ashley curtains while Wunderwear would come as she usually did looking like a Russian Shot-putter about to compete.

At least neither of them thought Wunderwear to be much competition which was why they kept her in the frame.

They chose a more secluded dimly lit corner. Thought it to be more intimate.

That evening they tried to remain calm, contrived to arrive late and attempted to appear nonchalant. They were also determined to stay sober.

They failed.

They arrived early and kept giggling at every remark even if serious.

"What do you think they'll be wearing?" asked Naomi.

"Leotards I hope," said Wunderwear, which caused gales of laughter.

They were by now well into their second bottle of Chardonnay.

"I hope they turn up soon," said Fiona.

"Oh he'll turn up all right, I just wriggle against him and he turns up immediately," chuckled Naomi.

"That I want to see. Dare you to do a lap dance as soon as he sits down, then jump up so we can see if he turns up," Wunderwear said with a fierce gleam of anticipation.

"Not in public darling, not in public," Naomi said coyly. "Wow, here they are, only half an hour late. Told you he was eager."

"Bloody Norah, they're both gorgeous, which one's mine?"

"Bloody Norah, they are both gorgeous, which one's mine?" asked Fiona hungrily, in fact almost drooling.

"Ours dear, ours," Wunderwear corrected her, equally drooling.

The two guys did look good.

They were tall, dark and handsome just like the sloppy romantic novels.

They introduced themselves as Wayne and Rocky.

"Yeah," Wunderwear thought, "they would wouldn't they? This could go swiftly down hill."

Wayne sat down next to Naomi and started intimately playing with her hands.

Rocky sat down between Wunderwear and Fiona and immediately started playing with his.

"What! Are you nervous, nah, can't be?" asked Wunderwear.

"He is nervous," said Wayne, "he's been through a lot lately but doing well now aren't you Rocky?"

"Yeah I'm okay I suppose," Rocky said a bit morosely, looking down at the table.

"Nothing serious I hope?" said Wunderwear.

"Serious enough. He found out his long term partner had been shagging his friends for years. When he went out they went in. Not good!" Wayne said sympathetically.

"Oh you poor thing," Fiona said, dramatically catching up his hands and pulling them to her breast.

Wunderwear although beaten to the punch recovered swiftly. After all Fiona was not exactly that well endowed. Good body but not much of it.

She snatched his hands away and literally buried them between her more than ample cleavage managing to smile sweetly at him and smirking at Fiona at the same time.

Fiona was not daft enough to get into a slugging match with Wunderwear so she deftly changed direction.

Rocky's hands were tied up in Wunderwear's breasts where he seemed content to let Wunderwear gently move them around in a caressing fashion.

Fiona struck. She started by placing her hands on his knees but quickly moved up to his thighs and somehow ended up well into his crotch.

"Oh you poor thing," she said again but this time a little breathlessly, her hands fluttering about like wings.

Rocky sensibly appeared unmoved. He hadn't uttered a single word yet was getting a right going over. He did grunt once or twice.

Wunderwear responded. She opened up his hands, slipped them up inside her top and helped him caress her breasts all the way to her nipples which she was pleased to find stood erect straight away. She noted that his fingers responded.

Fiona worked away even harder between his legs.

Both girls looked daggers at each other.

Rocky never said a word.

But Naomi did.

"What are you doing?" she exclaimed with horror, "for goodness sake behave yourselves. Stop that immediately."

They did and Rocky looked daggers at Naomi. He still didn't say a word.

"What are you doing?" she exclaimed with horror?

"Wayne has been telling me he's been to hell and back, haven't you Wayne?" said Naomi digging him in the ribs.

"Yeah," said Wayne, "sort of."

Fiona and Wunderwear were sorting themselves out and Rocky looked even more moody than before so they were all glad of a diversion.

"Do tell then," said Fiona.

Wunderwear thought, "here it comes again. I bet it all started with child abuse, it's the flavour of the decade that one. The media love it and fall for it every time. So what's new. The media fall for everything all the time. Okay let's hear your version buddy."

"Well I hate to say it but I was abused as a child," said Wayne disconsolately.

"I knew it, I just knew it," shrieked Wunderwear, then looked about her embarrassed and said, "whoops sorry."

"Carry on Wayne," said Naomi sympathetically, "take no notice of Miss Heartless over there. We understand don't we Fiona?"

Fiona was still trying, out of sight, to get a hold on Rocky, who moved in his seat obligingly, and so just nodded a bit abstractedly.

"Dad sent us to boarding school after he got angry with Mummy and Nanny over bath time."

Naomi and Wunderwear quickly moved to the edge of their seats, Fiona seemed occupied elsewhere. "What made him angry over bath time?" they both exclaimed at the same time.

"Dunno really, but it upset Dad, he was 'specially angry at Nanny," he said. Naomi and Wunderwear were all agog. "What happened to Nanny?" they asked.

"Nothing actually, Dad suggested he take the place of me and my brother.

He seemed a much happier sort of chap after that for a while. Then later Mummy had a baby girl and Nanny had a boy and she stayed to look after them both. Dad was never quite as happy again though."

"Come on Wayne, give us the detail? You can tell us, we won't say a word to anyone," they lied.

So Wayne did. It took ten minutes.

At the end Wunderwear's jaw had dropped, Naomi's eyes were glazed and there was dead silence.

"So you didn't have five little yellow rubber ducks that went quack when you squeezed them," asked Wunderwear plaintively.

"No, why, did you?" said Wayne looking puzzled.

"Yeah," said Wunderwear, "still got 'em actually."

"Anyway the problem was I got expelled from the boarding school as well as matron. She was a bit old though," said Wayne, warming up to his memories. "I continued my studies with her for a couple of years but got thrown out when she found someone younger. I was devastated and I have only just recently recovered actually."

"How long ago was all that?" asked Wunderwear.

"About fifteen years I think," answered Wayne.

"Jesus Christ, you need a long recovery period don't you," shouted Wunderwear, "what do you think of that Fiona?" Wunderwear gave Fiona a big shove which dislodged her from what she was doing. She gasped and Rocky groaned.

Wunderwear glanced under the table, looked at Fiona and Rocky and said, "you cheeky buggers, how did you do that?"

"Do what?" Naomi asked testily.

"Do that," said Wunderwear. "He was inside her pants and she was inside his trousers. They were going at it all turned on by Wayne's fantasies.

"They're not fantasies. Don't be so cruel," said Naomi indignantly, "Wayne has suffered, haven't you darling?"

"Suffered," shrieked Wunderwear, "suffered! Bloody hell if it was true then it was an adolescent paradise. Frankly it sounds more like a wet dream to me."

"Phew, you lot are impossible. Come on Wayne, come home with me and I'll show you what a young woman can do," Naomi whispered excitedly.

"That should be good," laughed Wunderwear, "can we come and watch? Pick up a few tips maybe. What do you think Fion'? Fion? Where are you Fion?"

Fiona and Rocky were disappearing out the door completely wrapped up in each other.

Wunderwear shrugged, smiled at Naomi, and quietly left. The friends met up again a couple of weeks later.

They were all alone.

"What's up guys? Not married yet?" Wunderwear said heartily.

"Married! married! If we married those two losers we'd have to be mothers," exclaimed Naomi, "they wanted mothering and smothering. They didn't want wives they wanted slaves."

"Wow, sex slaves, sheer paradise girls," said Wunderwear enthusiastically. "What!" shouted Naomi, "Wayne wanted to call me Night Nurse, wear a big pair of old fashioned bloomers, and beat him with a ruler. What with chasing him around trying to beat him and hold up the bloomers at the same time I was real turned off by the time he was turned on. We managed it at last and then he turned over and told me that there was a load of washing up in the sink and would I be a love and do it before I left. I really showed him the damage I could do with a ruler and quit."

Fiona then chipped in, "Rocky got very turned on when he saw our clothes piled up together, particularly our undies."

Yeah, what about that then? That's rauchy 'ennit?" exclaimed Wunderwear trying to get some enthusiasm going.

"Oh no," Fiona said very primly, "he just wanted me to wash and iron them and a whole lot more dumped all over the floor."

"Dunno that's so bad though," said Wunderwear, "You could always live out Wayne's fantasies. You'd be very clean, it would always be bath time. Can I be the Nanny?"

"Shut up, not funny," said Fiona, "let's have a bottle of red."

# Wunderwear Tries Hard

Wunderwear looked across out of the corner of her eye at first and then looked again more openly. Yep, there he was. Every time she went to the copier he would appear out of nowhere holding a few sheets of paper that never seemed to need copying.

Who the hell was he and what the hell did he think he was doing? Was he an office spy or something?

Nah! Although she held a responsible position in her company, she was a senior account manager, it was hardly the type of work needing her to sign the official secrets act.

She decided that confrontation was the best course of action.

"Take it easy," she said to herself, "don't be too rude, stay calm."

"Oi! You! Yes you. Are you a pervert or something? What you doing stalking me like that? If you've got something to say, for god's sake come out and say it," Wunderwear shouted, pleased with herself at showing such great restraint.

The guy jumped, dropped his papers and scooted.

"Right," thought Wunderwear, "this is a case for Human Resources, let's see what they have to say."

She barged through the door that said 'Human Resources' with the words 'Personnel Department' still visible underneath. "Those were the days," Wunderwear mused, "the days when words described what people actually did rather than some fanciful dreamed up description. The days when bins were emptied by 'dustbin men' and not 'Eco friendly Green Operatives'." She sighed.

She waived aside those wearing badges saying 'Your Friendly Human Resources Executive' and headed straight for the Manager's door.

"Hello Jim," she said heartily, "I'm being harassed in the workplace. Where's the forms?"

"Good Lord," exclaimed Jim excitedly, "haven't had one of those for ages. Are you sure?"

"Yep," said Wunderwear, "afraid to go to the copy machine, that's what I am."

"Well, please sit down. Do tell," Jim said eagerly.

Wunderwear told him everything.

Jim seemed disappointed. "Is that it?" he asked, "he just happens to be at the photocopier at the same time as you right? Everytime?"

"Well not every time exactly," said Wunderwear, "but often enough, in fact too often. And he doesn't copy. Just stands there."

"Sounds as though he needs help," Jim mused.

"What," screamed Wunderwear, "I need the bloody help not him. It might be not copying at the copier one day but who knows what might happen next."

"Well next he might not be not copying at the copier," said Jim thoughtfully.

"That's what is worrying me you dimwit," exclaimed Wunderwear shrilly, "if he's not not copying then what will he be up to? Answer me that then."

"Copying," Jim said sagely.

"Listen Jim, are you going to sort this out without violence or am I going to have to knock the living daylights out of the bastard?" she shouted.

"Don't do that, it's against company rules, you'd be lucky not to get fired," Jim said worriedly.

"Listen Mr. Human Resources, get resourceful. I am the victim. Set him straight. His name's Ted and he's in IT. Right?" She said, almost calmly.

"I'll speak to him, get his side of the story, okay," said Jim.

"What side?" Wunderwear asked making it sound threatening.

"Well there may be a simple answer," said Jim and should have left it there but he didn't. He carried on, "you may have imagined it, or over exaggerated or it may even have been wishful thinking. Don't worry, I'll get to the bottom of it."

Seeing the look on Wunderwear's face he decided to hop round his desk and flee to the toilet shouting, leave it to me."

The next day stalker was there, at the photocopier.

Wunderwear walked up to him but before she could speak he held up his hand and muttered, "sorry if I have upset you, I wanted to ask you out but I lost my nerve each time. Too worried that you would turn me down. So sorry."

"Don't be sorry, delighted to accept, meet you at seven at the wine bar and you can buy me dinner. Okay Ted?" She smiled. "Easy ennit?"

She walked off.

Her friend said, "you left him speechless."

"No," said Wunderwear, "he doesn't say much to start with."

She never prepared for dates, which didn't happen that often anyway. She preferred the man to see her as she was. That way there were no unpleasant surprises when he got a good look at her the morning after. The surprises were all up front.

Consequently Ted got a perfectly natural woman as a dinner date and seemed very happy with it.

The drinks were fine.

Wunderwear was starving so asked where they were going to eat.

Ted said that as he was a vegetarian, almost vegan, the choices were limited but he knew a place that made a great Cauliflower and Mushroom pie.

For once in her life Wunderwear was speechless.

She tried to get some words out but failed completely.

Ted mistakenly thought she was choking and started to slap her on the back and only just managed to dodge the left hook that Wunderwear swung at him.

Wunderwear was recovering.

Ted was defensive.

"If you think you can get a girl going with a vegetarian pasty you must be out of your tiny mind," she said, very aggressively, "I am very hungry and I need food, real food."

"But it is real food," said Ted, "Elephants and gorillas are vegetarian you know?"

"If you are insinuating that I look like an ape and am the size of an elephant then I think you are getting off to a bad start Ted," Wunderwear said ominously.

"No, I mean look, Elephants are strong but don't eat meat, neither do gorillas," explained Ted anxiously.

"Of course they don't you idiot," said Wunderwear, "elephants haven't got arms or knives and forks have they? They've just got a trunk for ripping up trees and two huge tusks that would keep their mouths miles away from the meat. As for gorillas, well they're just so laid back that they're too lazy for the chase. Sooner sit back and munch the nuts. Anyway they eat insects. So what's your excuse?"

"I can't eat living things," said Ted, "I can't destroy life you see."

"I can't eat living things," said Ted.

"But plants are living things. They live. What's the difference between growing carrots and onions, digging them up, chopping them up and munching on them and growing cattle, chopping 'em up and munching on them? The only difference is one lot walk and the others don't."

"Well we could go Indian, they do both there don't they?" asked Ted hastily, trying to save the day.

"I don't think we'd be very comfortable do you? Me eating one kind of dead living food and you eating another, but what the hell, let's give it a try," she said.

"I tell you what Ted, I wonder, if it could talk, what a raw carrot would say just as you were about to pop it into your mouth? I don't think it would be 'bon appetit' do you?" she chuckled, "and if I told you where some of my friends put bananas and cucumbers you'd think it a damn good job that they're silent. Don't worry they use lubricated condoms, safe sex you know."

Ted went a bit pale, excused himself and quickly walked off leaving Wunderwear alone.

"Wimp," said Wunderwear, "what a wimp, soon got rid of him. Now where's that Indian takeaway. There's Jonathan Ross on the tele tonight. Won't turn out so bad after all."

# A Powerful Woman

"You just have to meet Samantha," gushed Naomi, "she's absolutely fabulous."

"I thought that was Patsy," grinned Wunderwear.

"Who?" Naomi asked, a bit bewildered.

"Never mind," said Wunderwear.

Naomi briefly shook her head and carried on, "well she's brilliantly successful, runs her own business, drives a Porsche and got a huge house in the country. She's in good shape, head screwed on and got it made."

"We've not done so bad ourselves though have we?" Wunderwear asked plaintively.

Naomi dismissed the thought immediately, "what! what! You can't compare us to her. Don't even think it."

"I wasn't thinking it, I was saying it. I don't know about you but I reckon I've done okay," Wunderwear said more forcefully, "I don't have all that stuff but I'm happy enough."

"Except for boyfriends," Naomi said smugly, "bet she's got tons with others just drooling over her."

"Who wants droolers and who wants tons anyway?" said Wunderwear, "Mr. Right would do just fine by me."

"Thought you'd found him but let him slip away," said Naomi a little spitefully, "slipped off the hook, so to speak, whoops! Thrown back into the sea with all the other little fishes. Oh no! Don't go all dreamy on me again."

But she had. Wunderwear was a world away.

The girls decided to meet Samantha at the Wine Bar.

She was on time of course.

She flew through the door, took in everything at a glance, spotted them, nodded and came over.

"Hi there," she said, heartily, in the usual type of successful woman's greeting, "how's things?" Of course not really being interested in the reply.

She ostentatiously placed her special edition designer handbag in full view at the same time shaking her gold and diamond tennis bracelets down her wrist.

She crossed her legs with a sexy swish of silk and looked around to see if there was anyone else there of more consequence than her friends.

"Right," thought Wunderwear, "she's one of those is she? No sooner here with us than wanting to be somewhere else."

"I'm amazed you still come here, darlings, so drab, so bourgeois, so very wannabe and not quite there. Know what I mean, catch my drift?" Samantha said with serious superior overtones.

"You'll catch my elbow soon DARLING," thought Wunderwear, "where does she think she got off?"

Naomi however, much to the horror of Wunderwear, went all defensive, "oh don't worry, Sam, we hardly ever come here. We just thought you might want to reminisce a bit before we move onto do a bit of clubbing."

"The name is Samantha, not Sam, and I don't do common clubbing, never liked it," Samantha said tartly.

Naomi seemed crushed but not Wunderwear.

"You might have moved forwards but your memory's gone backwards a bit hasn't it?" she smiled, "I can remember you rubbing up tight against all the young studs at the Meat Market Disco. Quick enough to get their shirts off and even quicker with yours, no bra as I remember. They didn't call you Slipway Sam for nothing did they? A lot got launched from your dock didn't they?"

Naomi cringed expecting an hysterical outburst but Samantha looked straight through Wunderwear with an icy expression, lifted her glass of champagne delicately to her vermillion lips and gently sipped the wine before putting it gracefully back down.

"I have class now darling. I've moved on, you obviously haven't," she said, and turned to Fiona who had yet to say anything.

Fiona who had read the mood, went all submissive, "Where do you go now then, do tell?"

"Well," she said, very deliberately, "I used to have to entertain a lot but now of course I am much sort after and I am all over the place being boringly entertained. New York one day, Paris the next and then the Far East, so tiring. I am being nominated for Business Woman of the Year you know?"

"Yeah the Tories do that don't they, always the kiss of death that one," said Wunderwear, "fame one year, bankruptcy the next. What's your audit like Sam? Had one lately?"

Fiona was horrified, "don't take any notice of her Samantha."

"Does anyone?" she replied.

"Ouch," thought Wunderwear, "I'm not doing well here."

"What about men," asked Naomi very coyly, "bet you've got tons."

"Yeah," exclaimed Wunderwear, trying a comeback, "how many steadies and how many droolers you got in tow now then? Naomi said you were up to your eyeballs in them."

"If you mean do I have a man in my life, then the answer is no I don't," she answered curtly.

"Temporary of course," stated Fiona.

"Not at all," said Samantha, "you girls wouldn't know but men are afraid of powerful women like me. They are put off by success."

"They are put off by your mouth you mean. You seem to confuse rudeness with bluntness. It is possible to be down to earth without being downright ignorant. Why do successful business women have to act as though they have permanent PMS.

Seem to have been trained as bitches by Dynasty and Dallas and as for the Apprentice, well! I preferred the Simpsons and the Muppets myself. Seemed more real."

"Wunderwear, come and work for me," was the surprising response from Samantha.

"I need an outspoken down to earth tramp as a work slave."

"Wunderwear, come and work for me," was the surprising response from Samantha, "I am surrounded by boot lickers, especially the men. It would be a change to have an outspoken down to earth tramp as a work slave for once. I would pay you more than the mere pittance they give you at that Advertising Agency you work for. What was its name again, slipped my memory. Ah yes, Lies and Propaganda Unlimited, wasn't it? If you really wanted a touch of reality then you wouldn't work for the media at all would you dear?"

Wunderwear blinked. She needed a truce but unwisely decided against it.

"How did you get on so fast then?" She asked bluntly, "shagged the boss, did you?"

"Actually yes, although he shagged me really, in fact we shagged the daylights out of each other, wonderful, a great guy, loved him madly," came the surprising reply. "I started out as his P.A. and I'd still be with him but he was much older than me and died a few years ago. His wife got the money and gave me the company because she thought I knew more about running it than anyone. She was right but I still miss him."

"Aaah," said Fiona, "a tragic love story. Do you think you could love anyone else?"

"Not tragic at all, we were great together, had a great life for quite a few years. Not many can say that. Perhaps I will meet someone eventually but he will be a hard act to follow," Samantha said wistfully.

Wunderwear thought, "oh boy, everyone has a story to tell, even those who seem smarmy and superficial. It may just need someone to listen. My goodness girl, you're becoming all soft, sentimental and philosophical. That won't help your image will it?"

However she calmed down, went with the flow, ended up in a bar with a lot of smarmy, superficial people and enjoyed herself.

She didn't take up the job offer though.

"I'd rather shag the boss," she said to herself, but she never got the chance.

"Work hard?? Nah, I'd rather shag the boss," she said to herself.

# Twist and Shout

Wunderwear's friends were concerned. Ever since she had decided to save the world she had become more and more tense. She too frequently lashed out unthinkingly and often unkindly. They decided she needed calming down.

They decided that a Psychiatrist could be the answer.

They made an appointment with a specialist in personality disorders.

Wunderwear went along with it but felt that they should all go and have a bit of group therapy. Her friends disagreed.

When she entered the small comfy waiting room she found another middle aged woman already there. They smiled as Wunderwear sat down.

"Are you waiting, are you before me, am I too early?" asked Wunderwear.

"No," smiled the woman, "I'm waiting for my husband. He's just finishing. He'll be out in a minute."

"Is he cured yet?" Wunderwear asked, "is he okay? Does all this work?"

"Of course dear," she said, "he only cries now when talking about his parents instead of running away. Found him in Doncaster once."

"Doncaster," exclaimed Wunderwear, "my god, were his parents that bad?"

"Here he is now. It's okay Wally love, I got the box of tissues here. Dry your eyes now," she said, and off they went with their arms around each other.

The doctor appeared, looked at Wunderwear. "hmmm, yes I think I can see the problem."

The doctor appeared, "Come in Ms aherm, Wunderwear? Yes I think I can see the problem, Wunderwear is it? Oh my, oh my, do I get 'em."

Wunderwear made straight for the couch.

"Do you want the couch already?" asked the doctor, "we haven't started yet but feel free if you do."

"I do. Your lift is broken so I had to walk up the stairs. Need a rest, okay?" stated Wunderwear.

"My goodness, do lie down, I'll just call the handyman to phone the maintenance company. Won't take a second." The doctor flapped.

"Only joking," laughed Wunderwear.

"I can see there's more of a problem here than I thought," said the doctor roughly.

"No, no, the lift is okay really," said Wunderwear in what she hoped was a re-assuring tone of voice.

"I wasn't talking about the lift," said the doctor.

"Whatever!" shrugged Wunderwear.

"I can see from the details that you and your friends gave to my secretary a few days ago that you are suffering from stress and strain, correct?" asked the doctor.

"No, not me," said Wunderwear, "I'm not suffering, my friends are."

"I'm sure of that," replied the doctor, "so talk to me. What's bothering you?"

"Bothered, I'm not bothered, do I look bothered?" she fussed, knocking over a few props. A rabbit, a teddy bear, what the??? She frowned, "but well the weather's been lousy, my mother's not well and my sister's marriage is in trouble. Work is manic, layoffs are threatened and my friends are bitchy."

"My goodness, no wonder you are stressed," said the doctor sympathetically, "give me a few more details."

"Why?" said Wunderwear, "I'm not stressed with all that business. It's normal. I was just chatting like. That's all shallow, everyday stuff. Might not be for your sort but it is for us plebs."

"I see," he mused, "what is causing you problems then? All that sounds more than enough for me anyway."

"Yeah well it might be but I have really heavy things bothering me, like the World," said Wunderwear grandly, "not trivial rubbish like bitchy friends and useless relatives."

"Right," said the doctor, "can you be a little more specific. The World is a big place."

"I'm not talking about geography, what`s the matter with you? You got GPS for that. I mean the burdens people have that they can't share. How to feed a family everyday, finding somewhere safe to live, having a loving relationship and all the things that us fat cats take for granted,"

Wunderwear said with a dramatic downcast look.

"Can I ask if you feel burdened by guilt?" asked the psychiatrist.

"Are you crazy?" laughed Wunderwear as the doctor winced at the remark, "been talking to too many looneys have you? What have I got to feel guilty about? I'm not the one with two cars and three houses and loads of useless accessories to show off. I'm not shooting them or working them to death or humiliating them with unemployment. No sir! It's despair, that's what it is.

So what you going to ask next. Not mentioned my parents yet, have you?

Isn't that standard?"

"No actually, but it's interesting that you've brought them up, don't you think?" said Doc' a little too self-satisfied for Wunderwear's liking.

"No I don't think. I saw a guy leaving with his wife crying his eyes out that he can't go to Doncaster anymore because you made him talk about his parents.

So I thought that if you made me talk about my parents I might run out crying that I don't have to worry about the poor anymore. Worth a try pal 'ennit?" she explained.

Wunderwear saw that well known look of confusion crossing the doctor's face that she knew so well when she tried to explain her view of things to people.

She tried again, "why don't you change places with me, chill out and relax on your couch?"

The Doc' eagerly accepted the offer.

"Right then, I'll tell you what I think. My parents were great. Still feel great about them. I was spoilt but not a brat, well not much of one anyway. We've never been flush but never been broke either. They were still in love to the end and adored me and my brother, who's great by the way. We're buddies. I am both dependent and independent and I appreciate what I have so it's not unnatural that I should feel for and want to help those less fortunate and get a little frustrated on the way."

"See, you're great, I feel better already. You really sorted me out. Thanks, take care. Don't worry, I'll see myself out," said Wunderwear evenly and left.

As she swept past the receptionist she said, "Don't disturb him, he's sound asleep, probably needed the rest. He's under a lot of pressure poor fellow, bye!"

The receptionist followed her with mouth and eyes wide open but was lost for words.

Wunderwear reported her success to her friends, "thanks girls, got fit in one session and he didn't charge me a penny. Great eh?"

They recommended yoga.

Naomi had a new boyfriend.

He was into the spiritual side of life.

Wunderwear met up with him at her friends request.

"Oh yes," he said quietly, "I can see you have an outstanding aura, a large energy field, it surrounds every part of you."

"Watch it," said Wunderwear, not so quietly, "you can't see all my parts but you might when I get to know you better."

"Ohoh, he's getting that familiar glazed over look, better behave and change the subject," she thought, so she said, "anyway thanks. Still you're so fit I bet you glow in every nook and cranny don't you? Naomi says you get her nooks and crannies into the most amazing positions while Fiona tries all the time to sit with her legs crossed and her toes stuck up her arse! What can you do for me?"

The instructor looked as though he was going to say something but changed his mind.

He beckoned her to follow him instead.

He led her into a large empty room, squatted cross legged on the floor, composed himself and motioned Wunderwear to do the same.

Ten minutes later Wunderwear was still rolling around the room trying to achieve an upright sitting position.

"Haven't you got any bloody chairs in this place?" she panted, "this is a civilised country you know, we didn't invent them but we know how to use them."

"Why do you need a chair when you have a floor and your backside?" replied the man.

"Oh god, you're not very bright are you?" she gasped, "the floor is flat but my bum's not. I'm a rowly powly round bum and it's firm, not squashy. Go on feel it."

"Rather not at the moment," he smiled, "why not prop yourself up in the corner?"

Wunderwear did.

"Right," he said, "that's your first lesson. You have to find a position that suits you in order to begin to calm yourself."

"Well give me a chair then and I'll guarantee to be a whole lot calmer. In fact a sofa or a bed would do fine. I'd be calmer than a millpond. What on earth makes you think sitting on floorboards induces calmness?" she asked.

"Because you must learn to ignore your surroundings, discard comfort and retreat into your mind. Earthly things distract you from the spiritual," he replied.

"Right, okay then," said Wunderwear, "what spirit are you going to conjure up. Who's your guide in the spiritual world? Is it a red indian or what? Is it a spooky vampire or a Salem witch? I know, it's Ghenghis Khan."

"At this moment in time I wish it was," he said fervently, "however I don't think you've quite got to grips with this. This is not a seance and we are not spiritualists. Yoga is an art, a very ancient one of greater understanding through introspection and self knowledge."

"I'm sorry, you're right. I haven't got to grips with this. I have lived with myself since birth you know, never been apart from me, so I happen to know me better than anyone or anything else. I want to know more about what goes on out there than in here. So you tell me why I have to hide inside myself when what's inside is just screaming to get out."

"Truthfully I can't," he smiled, "I don't think this is for you, is it? It suits some but not others. Frankly, and I'm not being rude, you are more suited to be a cheerleader. You could frequently let it all out then."

"Yeah, I know," said Wunderwear disconsolately, "did all that. The trouble is I got lost in the routines and the lovelies nearest to me were knocked about a bit, especially when I really got with the beat. It took four or five jocks to carry me away and calm me down and even then I was still trying to wave my pom-poms."

"Tell me, is it really necessary to get to know things by putting your legs behind your head or standing on one foot for hours. I mean what does it prove when a so called Guru sits on top of a poll for hours other than he's a bit soft in the head, hard in the bum, and so are those who encourage him?

They're just showing off. If that's all they've discovered then they didn't have much to find in the first place," she exclaimed.

"Well I will get Fiona to sort out her toes and Naomi to seal up her nooks and crannies but to be truthful I don't think they've got much inside to reveal. You, however I would love to tangle up and then unravel," he grinned.

"Wow! Now you're talking. Okay, then let's get spiritual, come on get inside me and I don't care if we do roll all over the floor," she laughed happily, "who wants to be calm when we can come instead?! Is there anyone around, can anyone hear us?"

"Yes, but who cares?" he said, "come to Ghenghis."

The next day her friends wanted to know how she did.

"Fine," she said, "he really managed to get inside me, very deep inside," a delightful shiver went through her at the thought, "we went through all the positions and ended up with the 'lotus'."

"Isn't that the first one," asked Naomi.

"Not the way we did it," laughed Wunderwear.

Naomi was suspicious. The Guru was supposed to be her boyfriend.

"What exactly was it you did do?" she asked somewhat aggressively.

"Don't worry darling, a lot didn't have a name, but not to worry. He might get round to showing you when he's recovered. He's not really into nooks and crannies though, and I shouldn't try to stick my toes up my arse if I were you Fiona. You might get stuck and you wouldn't be able to get your bus fare out of your pocket and god only knows what a taxi driver would think if we had to carry you out using two poles stuck under your armpits.

"We did it all, who needs the Lotus Position?"

Her friends' mouths dropped open and Wunderwear decided to beat a hasty retreat before the angry uproar came that was sure to follow her unhelpful remarks.

# Out of the Blue

Wunderwear couldn't wait. The time would not go quick enough. She had an advertising pitch to make to clients before she finished work and could charge off to the wine bar to meet her friends Naomi and Fiona.

She felt it was a crummy advert anyway. The client brief was tight allowing for little creativity on the agency's part which was always bad news. Why pay good money to a top professional agency and then dictate what they should do?

Okay, the creative side was always a pain in the arse, with its drama and pompous behaviour but it was generally good at what it did. So let it loose on a project. Most did.

Not this lot. They wanted to go retro but not in a smart tongue in cheek way. They were a mouthwash and toothpaste company. The brief was for a pseudo medic to stop young girls in public places and ask them about their dental hygiene and invite them to take a before and after bacteria test. It was to be done apparently on the spot and in all seriousness. There had to be logos, product and packaging dumped all over the place in case the public didn't get the message.

Early results from the takes were not wholly successful. Five girls just shoved past, three attacked the cheesy interviewer, calling him a pervert and two more filed for sexual harassment. Three men tried to muscle in complaining of sexism. One had such rotten teeth that one of the camera crew told him to piss off as he was killing all the bacteria.

Only one girl agreed and she had to be restrained from wanting to kiss the interviewer with full tongues breathlessly asking him if he thought she suffered from halitosis. He didn't know what it meant so she was pushed out a little roughly and then placated with a hundred dollar bill as she threatened to go to the police.

They decided to do the whole thing with actors on an indoor set. It lacked authenticity and the clients noticed.

They wanted to know how it could be improved and Wunderwear was just bursting to tell them but wisely held back.

She suggested that the agency should present its own take on it and then they could compare.

To Wunderwear's great relief they agreed.

She packed up, briefed the team back at the agency and flew off to her rendezvous with her friends.

Oh boy, did she have news for them.

She was so eager she arrived far too early and had to sit for an hour wriggling her backside around on her seat growing more and more impatient.

By the time her friends arrived she was fairly hopping about ready to shout her news halfway across the winebar but stopped dead when she saw that Samantha was with them.

"Shit," Wunderwear said to herself, "lousy timing. What does that supercilious bitch want now of all times?"

However she was all smiles, "hello ladies and Sam," she said, "how are you today. Shagged any more bosses to death Sam or are you thinking of taking a Sabbatical?"

Fiona and Naomi glared at her in horror but they needn't have worried. Sam was on form.

"Wunderwear darling," she cooed sweetly, "I know you are a bit senile but the name is Samantha dear, try to remember. Nice of you to ask but my tycoons of late have been very young and virile and they have shagged me out of my tiny but brilliant mind. How about you? You're doing nothing I suppose and nothings doing you as usual?"

This was Wunderwear's cue, presented on a plate by none other than her arch enemy.

"Actually I have news," she said quietly and smugly, "news from across the pond."

"What pond? St. James Park or Hyde Park or your garden pond," asked Samantha.

"Oh nothing like that, none of your small fry. I mean the big pond where the big fish swim. Really big fish," said Wunderwear triumphantly. "I have had a letter, complete with air tickets, inviting me to stay forever if need be, so what do you think of that?"

"What is she burbling on about," asked Samantha testily. She was always irritated if someone else dominated the conversation.

"I think it's to do with her rugged fisherman in Miami," ventured Fiona.

"So she's a fisherman's friend," chuckled Samantha, "what's she going to do, suck on it all night?"

"No girl, not all night but for the rest of my life," screamed Wunderwear excitedly, "he wants me to stay."

"What!" exclaimed Naomi, "you mean go for good, like in emigrate. Are you for real, girl?"

"Yeah," she cried, "he said that if I can't get a green card then we'll just have to get married."

"But you were only with him one day and a night, weren't you," asked Naomi looking hot, bothered and bewildered all at the same time.

"Yeeeah, but what a night," said Wunderwear dreamily, "we wouldn't get spliced straight off though I don't think. We'd probably wait a day or two to let me get over jet lag. We've been talking everyday on Skype and Facebook for a few months now. He says we're lifelong buddies already."

"You can't mean you are actually going?" Fiona asked.

"Guys, I'm going. I tell you I am going," stated Wunderwear firmly.

"What, to a fisherman`s shack on a deserted beach? How romantic. I thought you had a bit better taste and style than that, not much more to be true, but a bit more," said Samantha haughtily. "Huh, a fishwife! just about right I suppose. You've got the mouth for it."

"What is she burbling on about?" she asked testily.

"A condo actually, on Miami beach," said Wunderwear, "he owns a small fleet of boats and a small processing and canning factory. He supplies dozens of shops and restaurants throughout Florida. Drivers do daily deliveries in his refrigerator vans. He just uses his own cruiser for personal fun and to keep in touch with the sea." She then giggled and said shyly, "I was his personal fun and he kept in touch with me alright. He wants to expand with a partner and he thinks I am an expanding partner. Good eh? Her friends were dumbstruck."

Naomi managed to mumble, "when are you going?"

"I have already given a months notice at the agency and the bastards want me to work it," she grumbled, "so I suppose it will be in five weeks or so. There you are, then I'll be up and gone. Don't worry guys, you can always come and stay. There's plenty of room in the condo. There's two Olympic swimming pools, tennis and squash courts and a huge gym. The beach is a few minutes away. Jesus, I sound like a travel brochure, but you get the drift don't you. I include you as well Sam, my partner will see through you in five minutes, but don't worry too much, you can always go visiting, keep out the way like. Don`t bother to bring that short arse hairless, neurotic pooch of yours though will you. You could always put it into one of those doggy hotels except that it doesn't much look like a dog. A Pitbull wouldn`t even consider it much of a breakfast."

She stood up majestically, nodded to them gracefully and said kindly, "well I'll be off then, lot's to do, I'll see you before I go, do stay in touch," and she swept almost daintily out of the door.

Her friends couldn't wait for her to disappear before starting to gossip.

They were disbelieving and nitpicking.

They didn't believe she could or would do it—but she did.

Five weeks later she had had her garage sale, shipped what she needed by Allied Pickfords to Miami, moved into a hotel for a few nights, had a leaving party and went.

# Really the Blues and All that Jazz

Wunderwear wondered what her reception would be like. Facebook was all very well but face to face was something else.

She needn't have worried. There in arrivals at Miami airport was a small crowd with a big sign which said,

'Kong welcomes Faye.'

Come climb my Tower with Me

Marry me Isabel

Marry your man Lancelot

As soon as he saw her Lance ran out from the crowd, swept her up in his arms, spun round, pointed at the banner and said, "What do you think my darling, do you like it?"

Without thinking Isabel replied, "yes."

"She said yes, she said yes," shouted Lance and the whole crowd cheered and cried congratulations.

Isabel blinked, tried to explain but thought, "oh what the hell, it's about time I chucked Ms. Wunderwear out and brought in Mrs. Isabel."

"You have slimmed a bit since we last met," he said, "looks good but don't go too far. I fell in love with a woman who I could really get a hold of and who really got a hold on me. No matter what size you were you always looked like an hourglass and never like a pear. You are a gorgeous whole lotta woman and I can't wait to get at you again. Whadya think?"

"Where's the bed?" exclaimed Isabel, "I fancy a waterbed, to make you feel at home."

"That's my gal, didn't I tell you people? She's fantastic," he cried.

The crowd agreed and cracked open a few bottles of champagne. No glasses, just straight out of the bottle.

Isabel Wunderwear felt at home.

No smarmy pretentiousness here, she would leave that behind in London and New York.

They got to know each other very quickly as they never stopped talking.

They decided on a quiet wedding in Las Vegas!!

Isabel was worried about meeting Lance's mom who sailed into her life one evening all bum, boobs, brassy and blue rinse.

"Jesus gawd almighty," said Mom, "thank goodness he's picked a real woman. You have no idea darling the one's he's hooked up with in the past. Hoighty toighty ways and no meat on their bones. Said they were soooo pleased to meet me when they sooooo obviously weren't. They thought I should be worried about meeting them and what they would think of me when I didn't give a brass bucket. You now, I heard you were worried about meeting me and what I would think of you. Good on ya. Well I reckon you're just great and if that lumpen son o' mine doesn't get you to Vegas immediately I will be getting my shotgun out and giving him a taste of buckshot to move his arse.

Now come and tell me all about that quaint little place you come from, England isn't it, an island I believe. So small how do all you English fit on it?

Surely some fall off the edge. That place Europe's your neighbour I understand. Not very big either, no wonder you all come to the States. I don't understand some of them. The Germans seem okay as most of them try to speak English but the French, well, I can never understand them."

"Don't worry," said Isabel, "the French don't understand each other either, never have done actually. That's why they have so many different governments and revolutions."

"Is that so," said Mom, "revolutions huh! well that explains a lot. They are revolting. They always seem to disagree with everyone everywhere. Don't appear to like America much. Strange considering they wanted all of it a long while ago. Just bad losers I suppose. Catch you later, enjoyed our little talk," and she swept off very grandly.

"Mom likes you," said Lance.

"Dunno how," said Isabel, "I didn't say much."

"That's why she liked you!"

"Are you a bit Spanish?" Isabel asked suddenly.

"What made you ask that?" he said.

"Well we're in Florida so I thought, you know?"

"Oh I see. Nah, we got Eyetalien blood. You know, names ending in a vowel. My full name is Lancelot Alphonse Vivaldi. Just like the composer but no relation. Do you like it? It's gonna be yours."

"Love it!"

"Well that's all right then."

"When will we go?"

"Go where?"

"Italy."

"Oh we go and visit relatives every couple of years or so. You'll get there.Don't worry. Why the interest anyway?"

"The lifestyle, it's great and so is the food."

"Hell! Don't eat the Italian food here, it's not like Italy. There it's a bit laid

back, you know, take it easy and all that. They have a great sense of the ridiculous and we don't all sing like Pavarotti, not even in the shower. The Americans love the idea but not the reality. They think we are all gangsters.

They never got past the Godfather."

"I know but the Italians have an eye for beauty, just like the Greeks. We Don't," Isabel said.

"We don't here in the States either," said Lance, "we confuse bling with beauty. As for love affairs, well, the Americans think it okay as long as it's secret. Get caught and all hell breaks loose. The Italians are amazed at the fuss. The guy here only says sorry 'cos he got caught, not because he's sorry he did it. The Italian says sorry but admits he wouldn't have missed it for the world.

"Music," Lance suddenly said one evening.

"Yes, so?"

"So let's go out not just to eat but to hear some great stuff," he said.

"Okay. When?"

"Now!"

"Oh, okay, where?"

"A club I know. Great Jazz. You dig Jazz?" he asked.

"I dig gardens, what's jazz? Is it George Benson or stuff?"

"Never mind, you'll see."

And she did.

They climbed gingerly down some spiral steps into a cloud of thin smoke wafting through the air, amidst crowds of people packed close together and an absolute blast of noise.

Isabel had never heard sounds quite like it. It reminded her of background music used in early cartoon films and movies of the twenties and thirties. But this was more intense and exciting. She wasn't sure whether she liked it or not.

The crowd wasn't exactly dancing but had a sort of unified swaying motion that was in exact time to the music.

Talking was impossible but no one wanted to talk anyway. They were all wrapped up in the music.

Eventually there was a break.

Lance turned to Isabel and said, "great ain't they? Real traditional Jazz.

These guys actually do come from New Orleans."

"Oh, right," said Isabel, none the wiser.

Lance laughed, "I can see a bit of education is needed, right?"

"Too right," she agreed, "I thought it was all 'Country and Western' here, but this isn't anything like that. This is wild."

"Look," said Lance, "to a jazz and blues fan this is it. If you can't play jazz and sing the blues then go country. You see the African American, when he was just an ignorant black negro, created four of the great art forms of the 20th century. Jazz, Blues, Gospel and Rock and Roll. Those supposedly inferior people who didn't know anything in fact knew a lot. Those supposedly so superior Southern Whites decided that the negroes were too backward and should not be educated because they could not be educated.

"These guys really do come from New Orleans."

With superior wisdom they then made it an offense to educate them not realising that if they couldn't be educated because they were so ignorant then why make it an offense to try.

So much for superiority. Stupid people. The states had to go to war because of white ignorance not black."

"Okay," said Isabel, "but what about the music?"

"Music is in everyone everywhere so the negro grabbed every opportunity including makeshift instruments and every sound around and combined them into something new. Jazz! It was a bit of everything coming out in a different way. The strange thing is that the whole world knew it and loved it but most Americans didn't. To them it was just black music but to the world it was just great music."

"Do you know that years ago there was this old guy, a creole, called Alphonse Picou, who played the clarinet in a New Orleans Jazz Band. He took a solo in the tune High Society where he made the clarinet dance. It became the standard, no one could improve it and hardly anyone at first could copy it. He even revolutionized the approach of classical musicians. Jazz itself, in all its forms, transformed the minds of the classical composers. All from these ignorant negroes. Ha fucking ha."

"Wow," Isabel was impressed, "when they gonna start again?"

"Shortly," and they did.

Slowly Isabel started to make sense of it. Listening to the Spice Girls, One Direction and other mass churned out organ grinder crap was no preparation for this raw uncommercial music. She wasn't quite sure whether she liked it or not but she began to appreciate it.

The band finished with a rousing interpretation of Dippermouth Blues, where the crowd startled Isabel by shouting out 'oh play that thing' at the end of the famous muted cornet solo.

"The band finished with a rousing interpretation of Dippermouth Blues."

Things cooled down a little and she wondered whether it was time to go but Lance ordered more beers and indicated that they should stay.

"Are we waiting for something?" she asked.

"Sure are, gal, there's a great blues band tonight and we don't want to miss it," he said enthusiastically.

"You mean like Eric Clapton or the Rolling Stones?" she said, on a bit safer ground.

"Yep, except these guys are from Mississippi not London. These are originals but they wouldn't be so respected if it weren't for your English boys. Your lot tried to teach America to appreciate its own music and are still trying.

To me it's a bit strange that out of cruel oppression the negro produced such beautiful original music and yet out of greater liberty they produced the ugliness and monotony of rap."

"Perhaps they didn't think too much of the type of liberty they got," mused Wunderwear.

"Well you may have sumthin' there," he said, "Hey here we go."

A young, well dressed black guy came on stage holding an acoustic guitar while a number of others were still bringing in amps and instruments and carefully setting them up behind him.

He sat down on a stool before a single mike at the front of the stage and without any announcement or fuss he began to play.

Beautiful acoustic country blues.

The songs followed one another smooth as silk. Fast, slow and mid tempo.

Bad Luck Blues, Before You 'cuse Me, Mean, Mean Woman, I Gotta Letter, I Done Got Wise and others.

Slowly other musicians were coming on stage, settling down and starting to join in. The blues singer changed his acoustic guitar for an electric model, no less than a National wired for sound.

He looked over his shoulder, slipped a metal tube on his little finger, nodded, stamped his feet in time and the band took off. They roared into the slide guitar version of Elmore James' famous 'Dust my Broom', followed by 'Death Letter,' 'Rolling an' Tumblin' and others.

Sensational. There is nothing in the world like a great blues or blues rock band in full cry.

These were certainly in full cry.

"Yeah, wow," cried Lance, "he's the King of the Blues."

He's the King of the Blues.

The blues band was followed by mainstream and modern jazz groups.

They left singing and swaying shortly before dawn in high spirits after a music saturated night.

A day later they left in a convoy of cars for Las Vegas.

They only sinned a little in the Sin City, found a small chapel and married.

They celebrated with their friends all over the town, starting with Caesar's Palace and ending around the Eiffel Tower.

They returned to Florida holding hands and probably lived happily ever after.

# They probably lived happily ever after!

# The End

Cover designs by
Danish Aikal Hayes

Author and Illustrator

The Hayes
Family wish
you all a
beautiful life.